WICKED SCHEMES

USA TODAY bestselling author

RENEE HARLESS

WICKED SCHEMES

USA TODAY bestselling author

RENEE HARLESS

TRIGGER WARNINGS

This book contains the mention of sexual assault, accidental pregnancy, and suicide. Please consider these warnings when proceeding. While none of the previous mentioned items are detailed within the novel, the author has made note that these topics are present.

Sexual Assault Hotline: 1-800-656-4673

National Suicide Prevention Hotline: 800-273-8255

I was broken.

Twisted.

Damaged.

No one knew about the childhood that had been stolen from me. I lived my life without trusting anyone and silently questioning every move.

The purple eyes of Haley Sinclair haunt my dreams. One bad decision changed her life, but she single-handedly destroyed mine.

A baby wasn't part of the plan, but I knew that it was my chance to prove everyone wrong. I feared ruining a relationship with Haley and moving forward with her would pave a path filled with regrets.

There was one thing I knew for sure - love couldn't be built on lies.

PROLOGUE
HALEY

I had no idea that cocktail parties for college students existed, but there I was, standing in a long black column gown that sashayed between my legs as I walked. The club our advisors rented for the occasion was in Barcelona. Spain had been the last leg of our study abroad program.

I glanced around the dark, wood-paneled space with a dry martini in hand. It gave off *a James Bond* aesthetic. Maybe I should have asked for my drink to be shaken and not stirred.

About a hundred students took part in the program during the semester, and I was lucky enough to be one of them. The students from their collective majors loitered together in small groups because we had spent the last five months in each other's company, nonstop.

Walking toward the art majors, I slowed my steps to not slip on the edge of my dress and spill my drink. I tended to be clumsy on a good day, but add in heels and a dress, and I was a disaster waiting to happen. Taking a deep breath, I did my best to hold my head high as I passed the other groups, noting how the men in some of the groups either cowered or gazed appreciatively. It was rare that I wore anything as body-hugging or revealing, but I had promised my father that I would try to come out of my shell more. That was our agreement for allowing me to take this opportunity.

I tried my hardest to ignore the women that narrowed their eyes or turned their noses up at me; females and I had never really got along well. My aunt Maria said it was because my body developed faster than theirs did and they were jealous. As a twelve-year-old, I'd had a hard time believing her and went with my father's suggestion that it was because I seemed mysterious.

Well, whether it was due to mystery or my breasts, my confidence always took a hit.

I passed the group of students studying foreign relations and then the lively gathering of English Literature majors. They were arguing over some author or book. I wasn't sure, but they had barely touched their drinks.

I felt the presence of one particular classmate as I walked by. I'd known him through friends and we had been at the same parties; heck, we lived in the same apartment complex, but he had barely spoken a few words to me. His friends, all cocky business majors, licked their lips as I shuffled by. But not him. He didn't even lift his stare from the whiskey-filled glass sitting on the table in front of him.

But I didn't want his attention. Right?

Finally making it over to my group, I sipped at the martini, letting the cool, dry liquid slide down my throat, but let the glass linger in my hands as I approached them. They greeted me warmly with smiles and waves as I took a seat, just as they had all semester. I was aloof and introverted and awful at making small talk. Instead, I found myself listening to their conversation flow around me.

The scenario brought me back to the going away party my old roommates threw for me at the end of summer. Everyone went about the apartment as if the Pope himself was leaving the University for good. But I sat on a stool in the kitchen corner and simply observed everything going on around me. The only person that had sought me out was my friend Keeley. I couldn't fault my friends, though. Their lives were changing and moving forward, while mine seemed stalled.

Pulling myself out of the memory, I glanced at my delicate wristwatch and noted that an hour had passed while I had been lost in my dreamland. Taking the thin crystal stem of my martini glass, I brought the drink to my lips and swallowed the liquid in one gulp.

"I'm going to get a refill," I told the group, but they didn't so much as glance up from their riveting conversation about the number of shades of blue. Now I didn't feel so bad about drowning them out with my internal thoughts.

Waiting at the bar, I skimmed my fingers across the high-gloss top, my deep purple painted nails following the path of the grains in the wood.

"How can I help you?" a deep voice bellowed across from me.

Glancing up, I stared into the darkened features of the bartender. He eyed me appreciatively and I felt myself tense up until he smiled warmly. Something about him put me at ease as he smiled and I gave him my order, watching him expertly pour the ingredients into the shaker.

My body tingled as the air thickened around me, making it difficult to breathe. At first, I thought the effects of the martini I had downed earlier were making itself known, but then I felt the gentlest touch against my elbow. Swallowing my gasp, I turned my body just a smidge to find Rylan resting his large frame against the bartop, facing me.

With a cocky grin and an air of self-assurance, he leaned toward me just as the quickly forgotten bartender placed my drink on the counter.

"Hi, Haley."

CHAPTER ONE
HALEY

Falling.

I was in a freefall, spinning wildly out of control, plummeting closer to the ground with each passing second. Nanoseconds. Life flashed in a blur as the clouds parted and brought me closer to my impending crash.

That's what losing my virginity had been like. . .a looming piece of my innocence that I willingly gave, not imagining the pain or aftermath that waited for me.

I knew that the man I had been with hadn't been of the same mind. He was known around campus as a playboy, but I thought we'd had a connection. At least, he made it seem that way.

Except, naïve little me should have known better. I was barely good enough to sit next to him on the plane as we flew back from Spain. The fact that I had been so easily forgotten was the crash and burn of my poor decision.

I should have known better. Bad things and I were like two peas in a pod.

"Haley?" a voice called out and I jerked my head toward the professor, not realizing that I had been staring at the wall to my left for the last ten minutes thinking about my last day in Spain.

I felt the blush rushing up my chest and cheeks in embarrassment as my classmates chuckled. Tucking my chin to chest, I let my hair fan around my head in a veil. That was my least favorite part about being pale.

"I'm sorry. What was the question?" I asked bashfully.

"I didn't ask one. You have the pile of syllabi on your desk to finish passing out." I glanced down and noticed that the stack of yellow papers rested haphazardly on the edge of my small desk attached to my stadium-style seat. Quickly I grabbed one copy and then passed the rest onto the guy two seats down from me, who chortled under his breath.

Great.

This was not the way I wanted to start the new semester. Traveling back from Europe, almost missing the connecting flight, and having classes first thing this morning was probably an accurate foreshadowing of the chaos in my life.

I was hopeful that things would slow down and that I could focus on finishing my senior year, starting a graduate program in the fall, or looking for a job. Dad had even agreed to let me travel across Europe this summer for non-academic purposes even though he was weary of my safety.

Tugging the edges of my open hoodie across my chest, I sank against my chair and tried my best to hide in the room of a hundred or so students.

I needed to focus on the information that the professor was saying about the course for the semester, but my mind kept wandering, and I was getting annoyed.

Men rarely captured my attention, to the point I wondered if my destiny was to live my life as a spinster. But this man had been different; my body jolted awake whenever I was in his presence, something that was utterly foreign to me. Even thinking about him left my body aching in places it shouldn't be, even though he wasn't in the room. I'd become accustomed to this reaction since I saw him two years ago. This wasn't a recent discovery.

Rylan lived on the floor above mine in our apartment complex, and when we landed yesterday, I was sure he'd want to share a ride back to school. It made the most sense, but when I approached him about it outside the luggage corral, he sneered at me and joined a group of women on the other side of the area.

My heart wasn't broken, there had been no love lost between us, but my ego may have taken a bruising. What little of it remained after years of teasing from fellow classmates.

Still lost in my own world, I jumped when someone nudged my leg to pass by. The class was letting out and I hadn't absorbed a single word the professor had said. I could only hope that there hadn't been a lecture.

Exiting the classroom behind the mass of students, I dove my hand into my crossbody bag when I felt vibrations against my leg. My palm connected with my shaking phone and I pulled it free. There was a message from Jolee, my old roommate, asking if I would be available for lunch. Checking the clock at the top of the screen, I smiled, mimicking the smiley face reply I sent back to her in the messaging app. I missed her while I was away for the semester study-abroad program. Catching up with my friend would be a nice reprieve from my daydreaming.

When we lived together, there had never been a dull moment. Wine nights, movie binges, and baking fests; the girls and I always had a blast. Willow was my other roommate and she was Jolee's cousin. They never treated me differently than any of their other friends. There were never any side-eyes or questionable glances. Those girls were honest to a fault. And I loved them dearly.

Willow was now living in Carson, North Carolina with her man, Eric, and Jolee was shacking up with Ford in their fixer-upper. Ford was a member of the Wellington University Ridge Rogues, a notorious group of playboys quickly reforming as they met the women who brought them to their knees. Three of the six rogues were already snatched up: Ford, Archer, and Chance. Link, Tyler, and Rylan made up the rest of the gang of adopted brothers. Dr. Tracy Fincher was their mother and a professor at the college. She was a force to be reckoned with on the Wellington University campus.

The roommates that had taken Jolee and Willow's spots in my apartment were fine, nice even, but I was happy when they didn't renew their sublease when I returned from my semester abroad. Instead, I took over the entire rent for the last semester of school until I figured out what I wanted to do with my life. Luckily, I had a trust fund and savings that I could tap. Music majors were pretty limited in what they could do after graduation. And teaching was not the career path for me. In front of a group of people, I clammed up. So, I knew I needed to use my money wisely.

There were still two hours until lunch, so I trudged across campus with my jacket zipped up to my nose and hands tucked deep into my pockets. The outskirts of Boston, Massachusetts, suffered through another bitterly cold winter, leaving a bite in the air as it nipped at your cheeks. By the time I made it to the social arts and science building, I had lost the feeling in my nose, and I was sure that my cheeks were painted red.

Fortunately, this course was entry-level and the professor was notorious for giving the answers to the exams in the study guides, so I had little worry about my daydreams affecting my work.

I sat through my philosophy class without distraction this time. Well, as little distraction as my sore muscles and triggered memories would allow. Except when the professor called Rylan's name, and there was no answer, I had to work to stifle my groan. Of course, he would be in this class; it was a newly added requirement for all graduating seniors. So, it seemed Rylan was never going to be too far from my mind. But I kept telling myself I would have to work at it.

As the professor droned on and introduced his TA for the semester, I thought back to my conversation with my father last week. He wanted to know if I had applied for the graduate program at Wellington or if I had decided on another route. He had dreams of me playing in an orchestra or symphony somewhere. But my stage fright would most likely nip that in the bud. I probably should have taken him up on his offer to enroll in public speaking classes over the summer. But I knew that my nerves would most likely stick with me for life. It would have been a waste of money as I tried explaining to my father.

As I glanced around the class, the stadium seats were almost filled, which meant that if Rylan stayed in the class, he would be lucky to find a seat. Though, out of the corner of my eye, I noticed a gaggle of undergrad females that seemed to be his cup of tea. They were clad in short skirts and cropped tops despite the cool weather. Those were the women that I'd noticed him with before.

Finally, class ended and I hurriedly packed my bag with the papers and office hours that the professor handed out, along with the business card the TA passed around, for whatever reason.

Jolee had messaged while I was in class that she and Ford were on campus at the sandwich shop and that she was ordering me my favorite turkey sandwich.

She was in graduate school while she worked on her Master's degree in business to open her wildlife sanctuary. Jolee originally planned on moving back to Alaska, but that was until she met Ford and they opted for staying in the area for now. She had already secured grants and financing for the sanctuary, and construction would begin this spring on the buildings. Volunteers from the animal shelter Jolee worked at had promised to help until she had things running smoothly.

Making my way through the masses of students and bodyguards, I trekked toward the food hall across campus. Wellington University was a strange place. Royals, social elites, and mafia heirs were among the scholarship recipients and regular enrollees. If there was a school that catered to and protected the echelon of society – it was Wellington. And the University had only been founded in the 1980s, but had been used for other "business" before then. Rumor was that a Mafia kingpin had founded the complex of buildings, but there was no documentation of such a rumor. Chance's girlfriend Keeley found a hidden room in the library last semester, so there may be some truth.

The school was on the outskirts of Boston, a small town that existed solely for the university. It was filled with gothic buildings that reminded me of old vampire novels.

As I entered the open area filled with tables and different dining offerings, I found the recognizable blonde hair I had grown accustomed to when she lived with me. Then I noticed the large group tucked into the seats surrounding her.

It seemed as if the small lunch date had blossomed into a full-fledged Ridge Rogue reunion. Luckily, Rylan seemed to be absent, and though I could breathe a sigh of relief for not having to humiliate myself in front of him again, I couldn't deny the way my heart fell to the pit of my stomach with a thud.

"Haley!" Jolee cried out cheerfully as she launched out of her seat, startling the other parties in the dining hall as her chair screeched loudly.

Jolee was by far one of the most naturally beautiful women I had ever met. When she flounced into our apartment two years ago, I couldn't help but immediately feel jealous of her blonde hair and big eyes. But I quickly learned that while she was gorgeous on the outside, she was equally stunning on the inside. She wrapped her arms around me, squeezing me tightly as if she hadn't seen me in years instead of a couple of months, but I couldn't deny that the warmth of her embrace left me with a hint of a smile. Jolee had one of the biggest hearts that I knew, which made her relationship with Ford all the more confusing at first. Ford was, if nothing else, an asshole to most people. But as their relationship blossomed, we all quickly learned that Ford was reserved for personal reasons and he loved Jolee fiercely. They shouldn't have worked, but they did. And I loved seeing my friend happy.

"I'm so glad you're home. I missed you." Jolee held me at arm's length as she examined me; her shrewd eyes scanned every inch of my body. Similar to how a mother would read her own daughter. Her keen eyes also narrowed as she took me in. "Something is different about you."

Trying to mask my alarm, I shook my head. "You're seeing things." There was no way she could physically tell that I had lost my virginity during my study abroad program. Hell, I barely believed it myself. But Jolee had always been intuitive; that was probably why she was so good at working with animals.

"Nope. Something has changed and I want all the deets. But for now, let's eat. Sorry everyone crashed our lunch. Ford asked if he could join, then it kind of spiraled out of control."

"It's ok," I told her as I followed Jolee over to the table and took an open chair.

Everyone started shouting their welcome as I unwrapped the sandwich Jolee had bought for me and took a bite. I tried my best to keep my eyes from wandering around the group, the absence of Rylan an obvious vacancy, but they continued to fall to Ford, who happened to wink in my direction. My cheeks heated at the gesture and I shrank down in my chair, wondering if he thought I was staring at him. Unfortunately, my eyes weren't drawn to him solely because he's Rylan's brother, his family had a direct connection to my own. But no one knew that part of my life, not even Jolee.

And if things worked out the way they were supposed to, no one ever would.

"So, we're thinking about throwing a welcome back party on Friday," Sarah and Jolee said in unison as I finished off my lunch.

"A party?" I asked hesitantly. Parties were not my thing. If you looked up the word wallflower in the dictionary, plastered across the page would be my picture. I didn't care to be around people. I was an introvert through and through. But I usually sucked it up when the girls had a get-together because it made them happy. And now that at least half of the Ridge Rogues were unavailable, the parties were less crazy than they had been in the past. Though the female partygoers made no mistake in letting the available Rogues know that they were interested. I'm pretty sure even Tyler, the youngest of Dr. Fincher's adoptive sons, had a woman break into his dorm room after the going away party at the end of summer.

"Yeah. Something small," Keeley emphasized. She wasn't a fan of large gatherings either, so she and I were usually off somewhere ignoring the drunken students.

"We don't do anything small, little mouse," Chance, Keeley's boyfriend, replied, earning him an eye roll while the rest of the group chuckled. I assumed he wasn't just speaking about parties as I had up close and personal knowledge of the size of Rylan's junk.

Junk? It's a freaking cock. Dick. Penis. I can mentally say the word penis.

Sometimes my innocence even surprised me. Maybe it wasn't innocence so much as it was naivety. I may have been an early bloomer, but I hadn't been interested in boys until I hit college. It worked well for my single father, but it meant I was way behind on the sexual spectrum.

"Will that work for you, Haley?"

"Huh?" I said at the recognition of my name and turned to Sarah.

"We were asking if Friday night at nine would work for you. We're just so excited to have you back."

"I don't need a welcome back party."

"Well, Rylan does. Where is he, by the way?" Sarah asked the group. I silently thanked her.

"Oh, he just got back from the hospital."

"What?" I shouted at Ford as he replied. The group looked over at me as if I had grown two heads. Asking about Rylan, or anyone, wasn't an everyday occurrence for me. "Sorry. I saw him on the plane yesterday and he seemed fine. Is everything okay?"

"Oh. Yeah, he gets migraines, and I guess he got one last night. Mom said he was out of medicine and needed a refill, but they wanted to run blood work since it had been a while. Plus, being overseas, I suppose they were just being cautious. I guess he lucked out with the first couple of class days; the teachers don't really give any work."

"I think he may be in my philosophy class."

"Did he seem strange when you saw him last? I know you guys didn't have the same sessions since he is a Business major, but maybe you noticed something?"

I think back to the slew of women that trailed behind Rylan in the airport and his quick departure when we arrived home. And how he completely ignored me on the plane ride home.

"No, he seemed fine to me. But we didn't really hang out or anything."

"Oh, alright. He just seemed a bit off when I spoke to him this morning."

An awkward silence filled the space and then Keeley did her best to chatter about everyone's upcoming schedules. Tyler, Rylan, and I were the only ones still in undergrad; everyone else was in graduate programs. The town of Wellington tended to suck people in and it was rare for anyone to leave, which explained why the small town was growing by leaps and bounds.

Glancing down at my gold watch, a high school graduation gift from my father, I noted the time and realized that I needed to head to my next class.

"Sorry to bail, guys, but I need to head to music theory and then music performance. I'll catch up with you later, Jolee."

"Sure thing," she called out as I tossed my bag over my shoulder and ducked out of the dining hall, her voice trailing off behind me.

A sense of peace washed over me when I made it to the music hall. My entire body relaxed as the sounds of instruments filled the air around me. This was the only place on Wellington's campus that felt like home to me, comforting.

Music had always been my solace. When my world fell apart, it was what kept me together. And now, I looked forward to losing myself in the melody to rid my mind of the last few days. I didn't regret what I did with Rylan, but he made it clear that it was just another notch for him.

Instead of walking toward the classroom where my music theory course would take place, I shifted toward the baby grand piano in the middle of the open-air lobby. I gracefully sat down at the piano, setting my bag on the bench beside me, and rested my fingers on the ivory keys.

Closing my eyes, I let the sounds drifting within my soul flow through my fingers. It's cathartic to let the music escape through me as if a piece of myself releases from its own personal dungeon.

I didn't linger long, just enough time to feel myself let go of the tension.

Claps echoed around me as I grabbed my bag and ducked out of the way. Hoping that I didn't invite too large of a crowd, I dashed into the classroom, thankful to find the room empty.

Tightening my hoodie around my chest and head, I went back into hiding, back to the norm.

Back to being invisible.

CHAPTER TWO
RYLAN

Regrets in my life were few and far between. I didn't have time for them, nor did I make myself available for those situations. Opening up myself to anyone outside of my brothers and mother would leave parts of me exposed that I'd rather keep tucked deep inside.

But knowing that I slept with Haley and that she was a virgin left me reeling. There was an ache in my chest where my heart used to be just thinking about it. I wasn't the person that should have taken that from her. I wasn't good enough or deserving of her innocence. But instead of staying and talking with her about it, I grabbed my things and left her hotel room. I knew the moment that the hotel door closed behind me that I had made a colossal mistake, but there was no turning back.

I hadn't even taken the time to consider how that would affect our dynamic. It would never be as simple as a one-night-stand. She was the best friend of one of my brother's girlfriends and we lived in the same apartment complex. We didn't run in the same circles, but it was inevitable that we would be around each other. I had been thinking with my dick, and now it got me into serious trouble.

On the flight home, Haley had tried to speak to me, but I did the ultimate asshole move and ignored her. I wasn't ready for whatever she wanted to say; I was too busy stewing in memories like finding the tinges of blood on my cock and the sheets, worrying that I had hurt her. Was there a part of me that was a bit smug she had chosen me to take her virginity? Absolutely, but I knew that I wasn't worthy of it. Sure, I was a complete dick to most people, and women only wanted one thing from me, but I would have treated her better.

The back and forth in my mind triggered a migraine, something I had been able to avoid for years. The pain was blinding. It was so bad that I stumbled from the plane when we landed, grabbed my bag, and headed toward the taxis. I had noticed the bachelorette party standing by their luggage as I walked by, but my destination was clear. I needed to go to the hospital and get checked out before the pain got out of control and left me blacked out for days.

"Hey, how are you feeling?" a soft voice asked from the doorway to my bedroom. Through the blackness of the small room, I could make out my mother's features. Dr. Fincher was my solace in the middle of a hurricane, a life raft that always knew when her sons were drowning. She knew that stress triggered the migraines. So, when I called her from the hospital after getting a new medication dosage, she immediately came to my bedside.

Classes had started yesterday and I hated missing them. Despite what students thought of me, I had always achieved high marks in my courses, which allowed me to participate in the study abroad program. Luckily, my mother was an advocate for me if I ever had to miss for health reasons. It had only happened one other time since I attended Wellington, where I was too incapacitated to leave my bed. It had scared my oldest brother Link enough that he rushed out of the apartment I was sharing with him at the time, wearing only his boxers, and ran to our mother's office on campus to get her.

"Hi, Mom. I'm doing better. I should be able to go to class today."

"Alright. Well, don't overdo it. You know that the first couple of days is fluff anyway," she chuckled. As one of the tenured professors at Wellington University, Dr. Fincher made her own rules and never gave out hard-hitting assignments until the add/drop period had ended. That happened at Wellington after the first three days of a new semester.

"Can I grab you some tea or make you some breakfast?"

"Thanks, but I'm okay. I was able to eat a little last night." Keeping down food was a relief because my migraines tended to leave me extremely nauseous. I always knew when I was coming out on the other end because my appetite would return.

"Well, I'll let you get ready for the day. I hear your brothers are throwing you a little shindig tonight."

Shifting slowly, my muscles protesting after spending the day in bed, I asked, "Are they now?"

"You know better than anyone that they need no reason to throw a party. Even with half of your brothers in happy relationships, the ladies still love you all."

"I wish they wouldn't, but you're right. The crowds tend to show up anyway."

"If you need to get away, you know that my door is always open. And I want to hear all about your semester overseas. The weekly calls weren't nearly enough."

"Dinner Sunday?"

"As always," she replied as she stepped forward and gently stroked my hair. Her soothing touch released any other lingering tension and I felt the effects of my migraine slipping away. She'd always been able to take away all of the bad and hurt. I watched her walk out of my room and listened to the front door click shut before pushing myself to get out of bed.

Sitting up, I reached around my nightstand until I found the switch for my lamp and turned it on, knocking over a book in the process. The room was blanketed in a soft glow and I blinked rapidly as I waited for my eyes to adjust to the change in light. I had an easy course load this semester. Most were classes that I needed for my degree, so they were likely to hold my interest, and one was an entry-level philosophy course that was now a degree requirement.

My body ached as I stood, bones and joints creaking as I went vertical. I was glad my migraine symptoms passed relatively quickly with the medicine —I was incapacitated for an entire week last time.

The apartment was quiet as I walked toward the living area, surprising me. Chance had lived with me before he and Keeley got together. I had been used to Chance making enough racket to fill the space, but since my return, he and Keeley had found another apartment available for them to stay in. Despite my offerings that they could continue living here. Keeley wasn't too keen on living with two adult males. Not that I could blame her, Chance was a handful on his own.

It also helped that my excess in scholarships helped pay for the apartment, which meant I wouldn't end up homeless.

After a quick shower, I tossed on my typical black denim and random shirt from my dresser, then grabbed my black leather jacket and worn backpack before heading to class. Except the moment I stepped out of the apartment complex I could have sworn that I saw Haley dash down the sidewalk at breakneck speed. Like she was avoiding me.

Was this the same girl that tried her hardest to talk to me yesterday?

Maybe I was mistaken. There were plenty of girls that had her long flowing black hair. Who was I kidding? No one had her body or hair. I could recognize her from a mile away. And now, I had pissed her off enough to avoid me.

That was what I wanted, though.

"Hey, Rylan," a sultry voice called out and shivers snaked down my spine, not in a good way. It was fake and laced with need, and I wanted nothing to do with it. I quickly nodded in her direction and then kept up my pace to class. If it had been any other time, I would have possibly given her my number or invited her back to the apartment for a quick roll in the sheets since that was all they were after anyway and I needed to get Haley out of my thoughts, but I had other things on my mind.

The Ridge Rogue groupies continued to follow me to the building, and finally dispersed as I stepped inside. I was thankful for the reprieve. My brothers may have enjoyed the attention, but that wasn't for me.

The morning flew by as I sat through economics and business management. I noticed that the few classmates that had gone on the semester abroad with me were staring me down.

"Mr. Richie, please see me after class. I want to speak with you about your internship requests," Professor Caldwell said at the end of class. He wasn't my academic advisor, but I looked up to him as a mentor.

Each summer, he and his wife allowed seniors to apply for internships with her business consultation company. I had hoped to snag a spot but lost out. Unfortunately, I was still without an internship that was a requirement for me to graduate.

Patiently sitting in my seat until the class emptied, I waited for Dr. Caldwell to give me the go-ahead and followed him to his office. Since he had taken me under his wing, I had learned a lot. He usually didn't offer advice to students. It was probably due to my mother, but I wasn't going to look a gift horse in the mouth. With anticipation, I took the seat he offered from across his desk and tried my best to mask my shaking leg. I may come across big and bad to most of the students at Wellington, but I was just the anxious ten-year-old bearing the world's weight on his shoulders.

"Rylan, thanks for joining me. I hope that I'm not keeping you from another class."

"No, sir."

"Please, call me Glenn."

"Okay, Glenn. You mentioned my internship?"

"Yes. Well, as you know, the spots you initially applied to have been filled. Unfortunately, if I'd had a say during the selection process, I would have made sure you snagged a spot. But the powers that be caved in and gave my nephew an internship along with some other Ivy Leaguers."

"Yeah. I still haven't finalized anything yet. I'm waiting to hear back from a couple of museums and an aquarium."

"Is that where your interests lie, Rylan?"

"Maybe?" I said, running my hands through my longish hair nervously. "I like the idea of incorporating education in whatever I do, but teaching is not for me."

"I see. I'd like to know how those work out, so please make sure to let me know, but I have another prospect for you. If you're interested."

He steepled his fingers in front of his mouth while resting his elbows on the dark walnut desk. It would come off to most as a power move, but I'd grown used to Dr. Caldwell's mannerisms. This one just meant that he had something important to discuss. Patiently I waited for him to continue.

"I don't know if you know much about music therapy, but it's a program growing with interest in our area. The university is interested in opening a degree program in this field, but they want some research done, specifically from a business aspect. A non-profit outside of Boston specializes in neurological music therapy, and they have accepted our inquiry about a partnership. I think you'd be the perfect candidate."

Just the mention of music makes my stomach churn. There are too many awful memories tied to music. Life-changing memories.

"Sir, I don't think. . ." I begin to explain, but Glenn holds up his hand to stop my arguing.

"Hear me out. You won't be there for any of the musical aspects. I know that it seems to be a touchy subject for you. I pay attention to other things regarding my students and you never come in wearing headphones or talking about the latest hit song. I've also had the chance to read up on you."

When I cocked my eyebrow in his direction, he explained that my file listed concerns from the therapist Mom made me see when she adopted me. I should be mad that the information was shared with my professors, but I suppose it's better than them giving me a project about music in the workplace and witnessing me having a breakdown. My reasons for disliking music were something I didn't care to explain to anyone.

"You won't, Rylan. You would be interning with the facility director, who has an MBA in business management. Various departments are interested in bringing music therapy on as a new major to the university. Having your insight would benefit you and the school."

He's right. The chance to intern in a field that the university planned to bring as a new field of study would do phenomenal things for my resume. As much as I wanted to do great humanitarian-type work with my degree, I saw myself opening bars or places for friends to relax and hang out, or helping businesses get off the ground. But I couldn't lie and tell him that I wasn't interested simply for selfish purposes.

"Can I think about it?"

"Sure, Rylan. Just let me know by the end of next week. If your answer is no, I'll need to open the internship to the rest of the students. I thought of you first."

"Thank you, sir. . .er. . .Glenn."

"You're welcome. See you in class on Monday."

I shuffled out of his office and through the stairwell until I exited the building, my boots stomping with each step on the metal stairs. It was too late to grab lunch, but I was lucky enough to find a rogue groupie randomly waiting for me outside the dining hall, offering half of her sandwich. I would have turned her down, but my stomach growled embarrassingly loud and I accepted. I wasn't a complete douche and never turned down a free meal. I thanked her as I shoved the still warm turkey sandwich down my throat in three bites, then kissed her cheek before heading to the entry-level philosophy class, secretly hoping that I could catch a catnap while I was in class.

I was fucking wrong.

There was no chance of a little shut-eye when I could feel the angry gaze from Haley hitting the side of my head from across the room. They were like laser beams shooting directly at me. She was here for probably the same reason I was – to graduate. But there were no doubts as to why she was shooting daggers in my direction. It also didn't help that the professor had already assigned work. This was supposed to be a bird course where students could fly right through. The professor must have noticed that I hadn't been in the previous lecture and asked a question while looking directly at me. When called upon, I gave a smart-aleck remark instead of the answer.

The room closed in on me. Despite my cool exterior, I preferred to keep to myself, though I never had any issues standing up for myself or others. I just tended to stay quiet.

"Mr. Ritchie," the professor called out as we began to exit the room. "I realize that there were special. . .circumstances. . .to your absence on the first day, but that does not excuse you of not knowing the material I assigned. It's up to you to follow up on missed work."

"You're correct, sir. I apologize. It won't happen again."

"See that it doesn't," he said in a nasally dismissive tone releasing the class. As if he thought me no better than a pile of dog shit that he stepped in, he rolled his eyes as I passed. Conversation over. I ventured out of the building, tucked my chin to my chest, and pulled the collar of my jacket up around my neck to combat the cold temperatures.

The walk back to the apartment was a long one, my mind already struggling with how to catch up in class over the weekend. I also needed to figure out my plans after graduation. I couldn't decide if I wanted to stay in town or spread my wings a little. But those fears would have to remain on the backburner another day as I approached my apartment. I was used to crowds gathered on the steps; it was a popular loitering point for the people living inside. Except there was one woman that stood apart from the rest as she sauntered toward me. If there were ever the definition of a Rogue chaser, it would be Mackenzie Lockhart. She was determined to sink her claws into one of my brothers or me. She didn't even care that some of them were in relationships. I suspected that she enjoyed the challenge. Unfortunately, I had made the mistake of sleeping with her twice already. She had this way of casting a spell on you and not setting you free until she was finished.

"Rylan," she purred as she wrapped one slender hand around my arm. Her red-painted fingernails stood out against the dark leather of my jacket. I glanced down at her bare legs. The skirt she wore barely covered her toned ass and the black heeled boots stopped at her ankles. She had to be freezing, but I guessed when you hailed from Hell, frigid temperatures didn't worry you. "I haven't seen you since you came back. Didn't you miss me?"

Doing my best to gently remove her hand and avoid a scene in front of the other tenants of the building, I faced Mackenzie and said, "I just got back a couple of days ago and I had some personal things to take care of. Now, I need to get some studying in."

Mackenzie stepped closer and pressed her body against mine. If any bystander walked passed, it would appear that we were having an intimate conversation, even though it was the complete opposite.

"I could join you while you study. And then maybe after we can do a little studying of human anatomy."

Taking a step back and then another, I apologized to Mackenzie as nicely as I could. She seemed like someone with a vindictive quality and I had zero doubts that she would exact some sort of revenge if she felt scorned.

Turning around, I nearly toppled over a student wearing black from head to toe. When they peered at me behind the hood covering their head, I realized it was Haley. Those dark bluish-purple eyes gave her away every time. It was the first thing I had noticed about her years ago.

Instead of saying anything, her gaze darted over to Mackenzie, then back to me, before she quickly skipped up the stairs and into the apartment.

With a heavy sigh, I realized that she had witnessed how my unexpected guest had been pressed against me and had assumed the worst. I couldn't even take a step forward without the world pushing me two steps back.

Should I follow her to her apartment and demand that she explain why she kept her virginity a secret? Probably. Did I? No, because I'm an asshole that was still angry about the entire situation.

But the surprise was on me because when I arrived at my apartment, Ford and Jolee were sitting inside and explained that they were throwing me a party to welcome me back. Me and Haley, to be more specific. It seemed like we were going to talk sooner rather than later.

CHAPTER THREE
HALEY

It's déjà vu.

There I was, a booming party going on around me, and I was perched on a stool in the corner of Rylan's kitchen. I hadn't even wanted to show up, but Jolee threatened to unfriend me if I didn't. There may have also been the mention of her burning everything black in my closet, which was everything that I owned.

Jolee did make an effort to hang out with me, but as the small gathering turned into an all-out college party, as I told her would happen, I ducked away and found a corner to hide. I knew that I could leave and she would barely notice, but I secretly enjoyed the people watching. I just didn't want to be included.

As I watched the bodies ebb and flow to the music in the living room, I couldn't help but feel my own music start to sizzle in my fingertips. I longed to find a piano or just the simplest sheet music to get the melody out; otherwise, it threatened to control me until I unleashed it. I had this personal straightjacket where the music would control every part of me until it found its way out. It was both a blessing and a curse.

Chance and Keeley arrived a bit later. They had to wait until Keeley finished up at her student teaching job. Sarah and Archer made their appearance just a minute later. Keeley immediately came in search of me. The distraction gave my mind a bit of a reprieve from the tune that was working its way through my synapses.

"Hey, Haley," she said as she wrapped her slender arms around me. All of my friends were gorgeous and slender, whereas I was the curvy one with a voluptuous chest. Something I'd been trying to mask since I was twelve and I woke up with them overnight.

"Hey. I feel like we just did this a couple of months ago," I said with a chuckle trying to pretend like I was enjoying myself as I sat back down on the stool. I hid the tired sigh that escaped. My friends had good hearts but sometimes didn't listen to what people actually wanted. At my going away party at the end of summer that Jolee and Sarah also decided to throw for me, Keeley had spilled the red punch all over her white shorts and pink tank. She was also homeless at that moment. Something I didn't find out about until I video chatted the group when I arrived in Ireland for the first leg of the trip.

"We totally did. Why don't you come out and join us," she pleaded, which surprised me because Keeley was a bit of an introvert like me.

"I don't know. I'm pretty good here watching everyone else."

"You're watching everyone else have fun. Why don't *you* have fun? This party *is* for you, you know."

Laughter bubbled up from my chest and I bent over as I tried to control it, my chest heaved as I tried to bring the air into my lungs. Once it started to die down, I looked up at a smirking Keeley, who had her hands propped up on her hips, attempting to be authoritative.

"I'm sorry, but we both know that this party isn't about me. It is one hundred percent for Rylan, who hasn't even shown up."

"No way, we're here for you, Haley."

"I'm sure that *you* are, but everyone else in that room? They are here for a Ridge Rogue. You and I both know it."

Keeley turned to glance out at the large living space and I watched her shoulders droop as she acknowledged what I was saying.

"Fine. I have no reason to argue with you, Haley. We just want to spend time with you. Please?"

I wasn't sure where Keeley mastered the puppy dog eyes, but she had it down pat. There was even an anime shimmer along her irises as she pleaded with me.

Sliding off the stool, I mumbled my agreement as Keeley joked that if I hadn't joined her, she would've had Chance carry me into the room firehold style. I couldn't say that I didn't appreciate her stubbornness. If it weren't for my friends, I probably wouldn't leave the confines of classes or my apartment.

"Haley!" the guys shouted as they lounged on the oversized couch or leaned against the wall. Females were draped on all of them in some aspect, but the one's not in my circle of friends ignored me completely.

"Hey," I said quietly as I followed Keeley to the couch. Chance pulled her onto his lap, leaving the seat beside them open.

"So," he began as he nudged me with his knee to get my attention, "tell us all about your trip. Keeley and I were thinking of taking a couple of weeks this summer to travel across Europe."

Before I could answer, both Sarah and Jolee chimed in and said that they would love to do that too. I could imagine the group making their way across the ancient lands and sharing romantic moments while creating those memories.

The sigh that slipped through my lips must have sounded louder than I expected because Chance immediately asked, "Was it not worth it?"

"Oh, no. It was. It was incredible. Even with all of the coursework, we still had a lot of time to explore. I can't even describe how magical it was."

From the other end of the couch, Jolee chimed in, "Were you able to write any songs while you were there?"

"Wait, you write songs?" Archer interrupted.

"When I can," I said, preparing to give more of an explanation, but then the front door to the apartment opened up and a gaggle of women poured in. I lost count at fifteen. But my eyes were glued to the entrance, the same as everyone else's. None of us seemed surprised to find Rylan saunter over the threshold with a cocky swagger that was all him.

"I'm back!" he shouted as he raised a half-empty whiskey bottle in the air. I noticed that he was usually quiet and reserved unless alcohol was involved, then he lived up to his reputation as a campus playboy.

Cacophonous cheers filled the room and the mass quickly swallowed up Rylan.

I couldn't help but roll my eyes at his welcome. It seemed as if he didn't even care that he had missed the first assignments in philosophy, work that surprised the entire class. Apparently, he had been gallivanting around without a care in the world. It must be nice. I'm sure he will sweet-talk one of the freshmen into giving him their notes to copy. Or they'll already have a set prepared for him.

I didn't follow sports, but between the hockey and baseball teams at Wellington I knew that we had phenomenal seasons in both. Conversations flowed back to the Wellington hockey team's explosive season. Chance and Tyler both played for the baseball team and they seemed to practice all year long instead of a few months as I initially thought.

Picking at the distressed hole in my black jeans, I twisted the frayed pieces around my finger on one hand while the other tapped out the music still flowing through my head onto my other thigh. Here I sat in a room full of people, friends surrounding me on either side, and I was utterly alone.

I felt a stare on me and looked up to find a set of dark eyes pinned in my direction. Even with the women pawing at him, his gaze never trailed away.

That penetrating stare that had convinced me he was the one to give my innocence. There in the room full of people, I was left feeling like a bird trapped in a cage, and only he had the key.

Quickly, I tore my gaze away and focused on the sliding glass doors that led out to a small balcony. The windchill was at a negative ten degrees right now. A few partygoers were loitering outside, but I doubted they would hang out there for very long.

"Where are you going?" Jolee asked as she pulled herself away from a conversation with a petite blonde sitting on her other side.

With a sigh, I flicked my stare toward the hall. A line had begun forming, which garnered a deep sigh of resignation. "Bathroom. I'll just use my own."

She nodded, then added, "Please come back."

I didn't reply. There was no point. She knew as well as I did the likelihood of me returning to a party I hadn't wanted to attend in the first place was slim to none. But there was still a chance, especially if I found someone to pique my interest on the way out. I wasn't completely oblivious to the male specimen. I still wanted to have a good time.

I navigated through the bodies in the living room as I made my way to the entryway, snagging my sweatshirt from the laundry room in the hall where

Jolee had placed it earlier, not even surprised to find a couple having sex on top of the dryer. I wasn't even sure how they managed to get up there. They didn't spare me a glance as I grabbed my hoodie, thankful that neither of their naked bodies had held it captive. Shutting the laundry door, I chuckled as I dove out of the open apartment door into the complex hallway.

We were lucky enough to have a nice apartment complex. The word was that some Sheik's son moved onto the third floor this year, so there was constantly security lurking about. Not that I ever felt unsafe at Wellington, but things could happen anywhere. Jolee was physically assaulted leaving the library when she transferred here two years ago. Thank goodness Link had found her before something worse could have happened.

A shudder passed through my body as I made my way to the other end of the long hallway toward the stairs.

"Hey!" a voice called out, and I hesitantly turned around recognizing it.

"What?" I asked Rylan, anger from him leaving me in the middle of the night and ignoring me on the flight home quickly morphing from a simmer to a bubbling boil. Had I really thought that I could move past it?

He seemed momentarily stunned at my harsh response but swiftly saved face as he unleashed his cocky smile as he swaggered closer. A sigh of praise seeped through my lips as he approached and I prayed that he didn't notice. I didn't need to add more fuel to the fire named his ego.

"Why so angry at me, cat?" he asked as he stopped a foot away from me and crossed his arms against his chest pulling the thin material of his shirt tighter against his biceps. I could make out each crevice of the muscle.

Confusion quickly overtook my anger.

Cat? Did he forget my name already? Confuse me with one of the girls in his harem?

"Haley? You look a bit dazed. Is everything okay?" My momentary lapse in judgment was broken and I shook my head slightly.

"I'm fine. I'm surprised to see that you could slip free from your rogue chasers."

"Funny," he admonished. "Actually, I was hoping that I could talk to you about something."

Immediately my anger returned. Now he wanted to talk, and I had no doubt that he wanted to know more about that night. Well, he lost that chance when he left while I was asleep.

"No," I said as I spun on my heels and began descending the stairs to the next floor. Unfortunately, Rylan followed.

Of course, the hall was empty despite the party going on above us.

"Haley, stop," he demanded, but I only quickened my pace, my boots making a thumping sound with each step. My apartment was at the far end of the hall, which gave me two windows in my bedroom, but now I hated everything about the distance.

"Go away, Rylan."

"Dammit, don't be such a bitch. I just wanted to ask you about the class notes."

Stopping abruptly, I turned to face him; his hard body almost collided against mine. It would have been laughable if I'd been an outsider looking in. Luckily he stopped just as quickly. I was glad because I wasn't sure I could withstand feeling his body pressed against mine again. It would only trigger the memories of how good his muscles felt beneath my fingertips.

"What the fuck did you just call me?"

One strong hand dove in his hair as he slicked it back. "I'm sorry. I didn't mean it. I just needed to get your attention for a second."

"Well, I do think that you meant it. You're an asshole; you know that, Rylan? An asshole. And no, you can go find one of your admirers and ask them for their notes. I'm sure you won't have any trouble finding a chaser to give you what you want."

I stomped away toward my apartment and silently prayed that he would go the opposite direction.

"Is everything okay?" Jolee's voice called out from the other end of the hall where the stairwell opened up.

I peered over my shoulder to find Rylan standing in place, his eyes glued to me.

"Everything is fine. I'm not coming back to the party."

"Oh, okay," she said, sounding disappointed.

Trying to better the sting of me bowing out early from a party partly thrown for me, I added, "Brunch tomorrow at Joe's?"

"Yeah, okay," she confirmed with a hint of sadness. "You coming upstairs, Rylan?"

Silence filled the space like a mist, suffocating me.

"This isn't over, cat."

"Oh, it is. Enjoy the party."

I entered my apartment without a backward glance and swiftly shut and locked the door. Leaning my back against the metal, I heaved a deep breath. Being around Rylan was potent. He makes me feel like I am spiraling out of control with no tether to keep me in his orbit.

Suddenly lyrics started to meld with the music I had running through my head all evening and that spiral transformed into a solid path.

An hour later, I stood from my keyboard and flexed my fingers. Scattered across the floor was balled-up paper, where I worked the composition over and over until it was just right. This piece would be perfect for my spring performance, the final exam in my music performance course. It's both dramatic and playful, an odd combination that somehow worked.

And for some reason, I couldn't help but notice that the music reminded me of Rylan. A battle between darkness and light.

As I read through the sheet of notes sprinkled along the page, I begrudgingly realized that I had a new muse. Rylan Ritchie. I'd been unable to make music that I was proud of for years – a writer's block of sorts. Now, the streak was broken. I supposed that there were worse people to draw inspiration from, but now I felt that I needed to do something for him as a thank you.

Groaning, I pulled up my philosophy notes and printed out a copy. At least this way, I wouldn't have to speak to him again.

With a quick glance at the clock, I noticed that it was around three in the morning. I tended to lose myself when I was working on a piece of music that wouldn't relinquish its claws from me.

I had already changed into my pajamas, a soft white shirt and a pair of worn almost see-through gray shorts, both items far from my regular wardrobe. I considered changing, but I figured most of the party had died down and I could slip into his apartment and leave the notes on his kitchen counter. I knew that I could wait until the following day, but with the music still fresh in my system, I wanted to repay him for his contribution while I was still in a decent mood. There was no saying how I would wake up in the morning.

Slipping on a pair of black Vans, I grabbed my keys and made the trek out of my apartment and up the stairs. As I suspected, the third-floor landing was clear, and Rylan's apartment door was closed. On closer inspection, there was a soft bass pumping from his apartment. Taking a chance, I twisted the doorknob and found it unlocked.

There was a couple in differing states of undress on the couch, but neither was completely naked. As I stepped further inside, I recognized Link, Ford, and

Jolee in the kitchen tossing cups into a large black trash can.

My friend noticed me immediately and left the boys to join me at the entrance.

"Hey, what's going on? Is everything okay?" she said with concern, and I immediately felt terrible about how I dipped out earlier.

"Yeah, everything is fine. I'm sorry about earlier, but I wrote a song," I added with a hint of a smile.

"Really? That's great." Jolee knew how much I struggled over the last year writing any music. I would sit down at my keyboard and agonize over the notes flowing through my mind, but none of it meshed well. I couldn't make it all blend, and it was agony. Like having a constant hangover without the booze.

"It felt nice to get something out that worked. I thought I had lost it."

"No way. You're super talented. Is that it?" She gestured to the small stack of papers in my hand.

"Um, no. These are my notes from philosophy. I'm just dropping them off," I told her as I headed down the hallway to the only room with the door shut. I assumed it was Rylan's.

"Haley," Jolee's voice pleaded, but I was already twisting the knob, not thinking about what was waiting on the other side.

Unlike the couple on the couch, the woman squirming on the bed was very much naked. She had her mouth on Rylan's cock, sucking it as if it were her favorite lollipop flavor. I couldn't blame her; his dick was delicious.

Fury surged through me as his stare collided with mine, but he did nothing to stop the woman from giving him a BJ or acknowledging that I was in the room.

I stomped over to the small desk and slammed the papers down on top of a stack of books sitting on the corner of the wood top.

Without another thought, I closed his door behind me and quickly moved down the hall to the front door of his apartment. I didn't miss Jolee standing there slack-jawed, but I was sure she would use tomorrow's brunch to grill me. I just wasn't ready for the questions right now.

As rapidly as I descended the stairs, another song came to me — this one fueled by anger and wrath. As much as I wanted to sleep, I knew that I needed to get the song out before it threatened to consume me.

Sitting at the keyboard, I let the music and lyrics flow, the notes and words coming together to make an edgy rock song. It seemed my muse struck again.

Fuck you very much, Rylan.

CHAPTER FOUR
RYLAN

I woke up feeling like shit. Not just because I drank an entire bottle of whiskey last night or because I had succumbed to Mackenzie's advances and let her suck me off, but because Haley had witnessed it. She had observed my slow self-destruction.

After Haley rushed out, I kicked my guest from my bed. I was only using Mackenzie to erase the memory of being with Haley, and that wasn't fair to either of them. But the sultry woman in my room didn't care. She was livid as she screamed and shouted obscenities in my direction as I handed her clothes over.

Once she was out of my apartment, I went back to my room and fell facedown onto my bed; which was the same position I woke up in.

I thought about reaching out to my brothers, but I remembered Jolee and Haley agreeing to a brunch today at Joe's. Wouldn't that be a shame if I crashed it and cornered Haley into finally talking to me?

As I tugged on a pair of jeans and a long-sleeved Henley, I remembered that Haley had left something on my desk. She left me her philosophy notes. Grabbing the papers, I couldn't fight the smile that lingered on the edge of my lips as I read. Maybe she didn't hate me so much after all.

I lingered outside of Joe's Diner in the wind. A light dusting of snow left white flakes on my leather jacket as I watched Jolee, Sarah, Keeley, and Haley sit in their booth eating breakfast. Haley's back was to me, but I knew that Jolee and Sarah had already seen me through the large front window. Of course, I was sure that Ford had told his girl that I was asking about the girls' meeting time.

I was determined to figure out what had pissed Haley off because if anyone had the right to be angry, it was me.

And just thinking about it spurred my fury.

Time was up. I opened the diner's door and sauntered over to their booth, standing at the end of the laminate topped table with a scowl directed toward the dark-haired vixen.

"Rylan, hi!" the girls greeted. All but the one who sneered in my direction.

"Hello, ladies. I hope you don't mind, but I need to speak with Haley. Alone," I said, laying on the charm. They might be my brothers' girlfriends, but they weren't immune to my appeal as a blush rose on their cheeks. I was also hoping to rely on their hopeless romantic side.

"Well, that works out great. The three of us have a thing with your mom that we don't want to be late to." Sarah looked over to Jolee in confusion but then jerked and nodded her head. I assumed that Jolee must have kicked her under the table.

"Ah, yes. Something about a vacation," Sarah lied.

Keeley chimed in, "Would you mind walking Haley back to her apartment?"

Haley stared at her abandoning friends like they had just killed her pet. It was fascinating. Those girls could really sell a story.

"No," Haley stated defiantly, but her friends demanded that she sat her butt in place.

"I just need five minutes."

"Fine," Haley murmured as she watched her friends gather their things, mumbling that they were traitors under her breath. Haley didn't acknowledge their waves goodbye; she continued to sulk in the booth's corner as if she couldn't get far enough from me.

I slid along the vinyl seating across from her, my large frame filling most of the space.

"What has your panties in a twist, cat?"

Her forlorn expression mutated into one of shock and I couldn't resist the chuckle that burst free.

"Excuse me? You lost the right to ask about my panties the moment you slipped out of my room in the middle of the night. In a freaking foreign country, for goodness sake."

"Ah, so you're mad that I didn't stick around. Cat, I don't ever stick around."

"Stop calling me that."

"No. And when were you planning on telling me that you were. . .innocent." I tried to whisper the last part, but it still alerted the group sitting across from us. Haley's pale cheeks turned ruddy in embarrassment.

"Thanks for that, fuckboy. And maybe I wanted it gone and I knew you didn't care who you screwed as long as it had two legs."

Talk about a fucking low blow. Haley knew how to hit so far below the belt that I bet Satan even gasped.

Her phone buzzed where it sat on the table and she grabbed it, but not before I read the name Eddie across the screen.

"Eddie? Who names his kid Eddie?"

"My ex, if you must know. And his actual name is Edwin."

"That's even worse. It sounds like he's a stuck-up prick."

"And you'd be right. What does that make me since Eddie and I dated on and off for the last four years?"

Damn, maybe I didn't know Haley at all. I couldn't imagine her with a guy that sounded like he slept on a pile of cash. Then it reminded me that she never trusted him enough to give him her virginity.

"You should have told me. I deserved to know."

"Why? So you could tell me no? So you could make some lame excuse that you didn't want to deflower anyone? If I didn't care, why should you?"

"It does matter! It did matter!" I shouted. We were drawing a crowd, and as much as I enjoyed watching the flush rise on Haley's cheeks, we didn't need to air out our dirty laundry in the middle of Joe's

Diner. It would probably end up on the University's messaging portal within the hour. "Is there somewhere else we can talk where we won't be watched and examined?"

"We don't need to go anywhere. This conversation is over," she said as she scooted out of the booth and stood, wrapping a puffy black jacket over her body.

"Like hell it is. We're finishing this. Today. Because I'm not finished."

"Well, I am. Do what you want. Follow me for all I care, but as I've witnessed, you're much better at leaving."

Man, she knew how to hold a grudge. If not just for our own sanity, but because she was directly involved with my family. I almost feared that we could never come to some sort of solidarity. We could hate each other all we wanted in secret, but we needed to play nice until graduation.

She stormed out of the diner, leaving a twenty on the table and I ambled behind her. I wasn't used to women leaving me; I was usually the one kicking them out. The change was jarring.

I expected her to turn left and continue toward our apartment complex, but she skipped across the street and took the pathway connecting to the university. The snow continued to fall around us as I followed her to the other side of campus. Her dark hair swung with each step, and the movement hypnotized me. God, she was gorgeous. Not one of the skinny girls that flaunted themselves around Wellington. Haley had curves for days and I had a feeling that she underestimated her appeal to men.

She began climbing the steps as we approached the arts building and I had to take a deep breath before venturing inside. I avoided this building at all costs, specifically the wing of the music department. My parents ruined any pleasure I'd get from music.

I was unsure if Haley realized that I'd continued to follow her, but as she entered a small room where a piano sat against the wall, she gestured to a seat against the wall across from her. Her puffy jacket and bag were placed on the floor at her feet.

"Talk if you want to talk, but I need to practice." She perched on the piano's bench and faced me. Her body was less tense and I assumed she lost some of her steam on the way over.

"Why didn't you tell me that you were a virgin?"

A long strand of hair draped over her shoulder and she reached up and began twirling it around her long fingers. The move was fascinating to watch and hypnotizing. I recalled the way her fingers felt sliding up and down my shaft.

"Because it wasn't your problem. It was mine."

"Well, you deserved better. You should have had someone take their time with you, treasure you." I recalled how I had pounded into her tight channel like a fucking jackhammer. How her body gripped mine so tightly that I could barely contain my load. Fuck, she had felt perfect beneath me. "Instead. . .instead you got-"

"I got a man that left in the middle of the night because I was just another notch for you, right?"

Standing from my chair, grateful it was against the wall or it would have toppled over, I angrily began to pace. This woman knew how to make me lose my cool faster than anyone I had ever met.

"No! I left because I freaked out. The thing is. . .I didn't want to leave. It was more, Haley. But then I saw the blood and I freaked. At first, I thought I had hurt you until I realized what it meant. Fuck, I am not the person a girl wants to give her virginity to. I have nothing to give. But no. You had to keep it from me to get what you wanted."

She stared at me from the bench, violence in her gaze. Those purple eyes narrowed into barely discernible slits. "Well, I'm fucking sorry it never occurred to me that it would matter to you. Maybe instead of running like a scared little boy, you could have waited to talk to me. Then to top it off, you ignored me the entire way home. I didn't even know why. You made me feel like a freak. Like I had done something wrong."

"You did. You lied!"

"I didn't fucking lie!"

"Omitting the truth is the same fucking thing."

We stared at each other, nostrils flaring, chests heaving as the anger in the room sizzled around us.

A skinny guy popped his head in from the room's doorway and asked if we were okay, but neither of us replied.

"Do you need me to call security, miss?" he asked as he eyed me suspiciously.

"No," Haley said as her fire subsided. She turned on a charming smile and faced the intruder. "We were just arguing about a project for class. Rylan wouldn't hurt me. We'll keep it down."

"Okay, miss. I'll be in the room across the way."

I sniffed loudly as I crossed my arms against my chest. Like he could do anything. I could snap him like a twig.

Haley nodded her thanks and turned her tired gaze back to me. "Look. You're mad about my virginity. I'm mad that you ran off and made it worse when I tried to thank you by bringing you my philosophy notes only to find that chick sucking you off."

"Jealous?" I taunted her.

"Absolutely not. I hate giving blow jobs." I snorted. She just hadn't met the right cock yet. I had to pry women off my erections the majority of the time. When I took Haley's virginity, we were both so lost in the moment that foreplay was the last thing on our minds. She was soaked the moment my fingers touched the soft flesh between her legs.

"I guess you hate being eaten out too."

Shrugging her shoulders, she walked back to the bench, removed her jacket, and sat down. "I could do without."

"Then it wasn't ever done right. I could eat pussy for hours."

"Good for you. Are we done?"

I moved from the chair and went to stand behind her. The black sweater she wore was cut in a low V, so the tops of her remarkable breasts peeked out. Fuck, I loved her chest.

"What did you come to thank me for?" I asked her just as I placed my hands on her shoulders. Her body flinched but only slightly as if she hadn't expected the touch. Her warmth seeped through the material to my palms, like holding my hands in front of a campfire on a chilly night, and it sent waves of desire straight to my cock.

"Nothing important."

"Oh, I think it was, or you would have waited. Tell me what it was, cat."

My fingers slipped beneath the edge of her sweater. I slid my palms down her body to cup her breasts. The rumble of her moan vibrated through my arms and I had to suppress my growl.

"Tell me what you were thanking me for?" I asked again, my fingertips grazing the edge of her nipples.

"No," she whispered and my cock immediately jolted to attention.

Leaning forward, I pressed my lips against the outer rim of her ear. "Was it for taking a piece of you that no one else has had?"

The sudden loss at my hands was jarring. She moved so quickly that I almost tumbled over the bench.

"No. I was not thanking you for taking my virginity. I was thanking you for inspiring me to write songs again. So please, Rylan, continue to be an asshole. . .it seems to be working in my favor."

Fuck. I had seriously considered that her innocence was what we were discussing, but music? That was something I couldn't handle. I didn't want to be associated with anything related to that art.

I wasn't sure how to respond. Thank her? It would be the nice thing to do, but I was an asshole. Ask to hear the piece? It would be like nails on a chalkboard to my ears, but I couldn't overthrow the curiosity that I felt. I'd never inspired anything beautiful before. My world was a disgusting wasteland.

Choking back the fear, I asked her if I could hear the piece I had inspired and I waited for what felt like hours before she sat down at the piano.

There were no lyrics but a fast-paced melody with a hint of anger behind it. It was fucking phenomenal and jarring at the same time. This was how she felt about me, about us. Annoyance. Rage. Infuriation.

But damn if she wasn't sexy as hell moving her body to the beat of the song. The last key lingered in the air as she spun around to face me.

"Happy?" she asked with venom lacing her words, but I was still in shock.

Before I could respond, my legs were carrying me over to the bench. I cupped her face in my hands and smashed my lips against hers. Haley's mouth immediately opened for me as she reached up and gripped my arms. I swiped my tongue against hers and I wanted nothing more than to lay her down on this bench and slide my tongue between her legs. I'd have to make that happen.

As quickly as she opened up, Haley pushed at my chest, ending our kiss.

"Get out, Rylan."

"What?" I asked her in bewilderment.

"I have to practice and I know that you have work to catch up on. We'll call a truce. Okay?"

"Truce? Hell no. I know you feel the chemistry here; otherwise, you would have chosen someone else to give your v-card."

"Rylan. . ." she said with a heavy sigh.

"Fine. Have it your way. But it's not over, cat."

I forced myself to leave her, regretting every step as I moved farther and farther from the building. The snow falling around me did little to cool off my body; the kiss we shared still had me worked up. But I had nowhere to go, no destination in mind.

Snagging my phone from my back pocket, I called my older brother Link to see if he wanted to hit up the gym. Normally I'd use sex to work it out of my system, but that wasn't what I wanted right now. I needed to burn off some energy.

He agreed to meet me in half an hour, which left me enough time to change and make my way to the small gym we used in town. The university had a top-of-the-line facility, but we preferred the old gym run by an ex-professional boxer. Ray was as cool as they came and he made sure that any rogue chasers that made their way to the site kept their claws to themselves.

I walked into the facility, found Link walking toward the locker room, and I followed. We stored our things without a word exchanged until we walked toward the barbells.

"Spot me?" I asked him as I locked the weights in place on the bar, then laid down on the bench.

As I began, Link remained quiet until I had passed a few reps. "Want to talk about it?" he asked.

Link knew me well. As the oldest brother, he took us all under his wing when we came to live with Dr. Fincher. He and Ford had been with her the longest since they were young when they were adopted. I joined her family at the age of eleven.

I wasn't sure how much I wanted to disclose to him, but I knew that I needed to talk to someone because it made the group situation a bit more complicated.

"I. . .ugh. . .I slept with Haley when we were in Spain." I huffed as I finished the last rep and set the bar on the rack, then twisted on the seat to look at Link. It was rare that he was stunned speechless. The only time he was ever quiet was when he was observing people.

"Um, Haley? Jolee's friend?"

"Yeah."

"I thought she had a boyfriend?"

Fuck, did she? She never mentioned him, and she had said that he was her ex at the diner.

"I think they were broken up. He called her while she was at the diner today and she said he was her ex. Fuck, man."

"I'm guessing that's not all." He gestured for me to switch spots with him.

Once he's settled and had the bar secured in his grasp, I continued. "She was a virgin, Link. She never said anything, and when we were done, I freaked out."

"Okay," he said as he pushed through another rep. "It's not the end of the world. She seems like a cool chick. I wouldn't be afraid that she's a clinger or anything."

"Yeah, you're right."

We didn't exchange anymore conversation as he finished his reps, but as he sat up, Link added, "You like her."

"Don't be a dick," I told him as I walked toward the treadmill.

"You do. I can see it. You're usually the first to brush everything off. Cool and chill Rylan. But you like this one; that's why you're all mixed up. I'm glad. I like her for you."

Is that it? Did I like her?

But there was more than just liking her, or that we had sex, I knew something that I wasn't prepared to share with her. And there was no way I wanted it coming to light.

We finished our hour workout at the gym and I promised to see him at Mom's tomorrow for our weekly Sunday dinners. At least I'd get a bit of reprieve before I had to see Haley again on Monday in class. That was if Link kept his mouth shut.

CHAPTER FIVE
HALEY

I didn't know that it was possible to ignore someone for a month completely, but somehow I had successfully avoided Rylan except for a few times in passing. I would give a quick hello or some lame excuse of needing to go somewhere, but I was still freaked out.

There were nights I spent hours pleasuring myself to the images of Rylan from our night together. Hell, even the way he stroked my breasts when he followed me into the music room brought me to orgasm.

He had tried to corner me after philosophy class a few times, but because I sat closer to the door, I was able to sneak out before he could track me down. I may have even ignored the knocks on my door the few times I spied him through the peephole. Any other girl on campus would be thrilled to have Rylan chasing after her, but not me. I feared that there was something more to his visits and I wanted to leave our truce where it lay.

Leaving the arts building, I passed by the business hall just as Rylan exited with the same group of guys from the study abroad program. A few of them looked in my direction, skeevy grins on their faces. Those were the type of guys that made me think they'd drug a girl at a bar. Rylan didn't acknowledge me as I passed and I was happy about it. The awkwardness between us was growing everyday and I knew it was all my doing.

From my bag, my phone began to buzz and I saw there was another message from Eddie.

Eddie: We need to talk. Now.

No, we didn't. Eddie wanted to get back together again. I had zero desire to be with a guy that had slept with half of the girls in his dorm behind my back. I guessed subconsciously that my body knew that he wasn't worthy of being my first.

Just as I began to put the phone away an incoming call from my father had me quickly answering.

"Daddy!"

"Hey, angel. How is your week going?"

"Good. Busy. I have a couple of projects and I need to begin rehearsal for my spring performance."

"That's your final exam, right?"

"Yep. But I'll figure it out. I'm turning in an original composition and vocals."

My father's startled gasp echoed through the line. "You've been writing again?" he asked. Since my sophomore year in high school, when a scandal had left my family almost destitute, I had struggled to write songs. It became forced and I began to hate it. Luckily I had so many pieces from before that time that I had enough compositions to last me until this year for my courses.

"I have. I suppose the trip triggered my muse."

That was putting it mildly. The trip was a catalyst. Rylan had been the knight that saved it all. Not that I wanted Rylan to dwell on that.

"That's great to hear. I'm sorry I haven't been around much. We've been working with another practice that is closing and taking on their patients."

My father was one of the top orthodontists in Boston. He worked on celebrities, athletes, and their children, giving us a cushy lifestyle; one that was tarnished by lies. My father was able to overcome the rumors, but my mother hadn't been so lucky. I still get choked up thinking about her.

"That's okay. I know you're busy. Do you think you're up for a visit next weekend? I'd like to have dinner with you for your birthday."

"Of course. I'm always happy to see you. There is also someone I'd like you to meet."

I was stunned into silence. It had been almost five years since we lost Mom, but it still felt like yesterday to me. How could my father possibly be ready to date again?

"Haley? Sweetie, your mom would want us to be happy and move on. I really think you'll like Gina."

I wanted to tell him that I didn't think I would, but instead, I bit my tongue and told him that I'd see him on Saturday at his favorite restaurant.

Ending the call, I realized I had wandered over to the fountain in the middle of the quad. Despite the frigid temperatures, the water flowed freely, babbling as it fell down into the pool. It was rumored that maintenance warmed the water so that it didn't freeze over. I wouldn't have been surprised.

Across the way, a group of guys, who I assumed was the hockey team based on their size, made their way to the on-campus gym. A cluster of women followed closely in their workout gear, but I had a feeling they were there to ogle the guys.

Students walked down the path with gloved hands holding their coffees tightly or typing away on their phones. The world went on around me. Everyone was moving on, but I felt stuck.

I didn't want to forget my mother. How she taught me how to play the piano at the age of four, bake by the age of eight, and compose music at ten. She was the most talented person I knew and she was taken from me far too soon. I still never believed the lies I was fed, that she had taken her own life. But all of the police reports stated it as fact.

Standing for another moment, I watched how the water fell down the concrete bowls, the tune a soft song. I began to hum along to the beat and an arrangement began to build in my mind. This was what I needed; the escape from everything to find my center.

The smile grew with every step I took toward my apartment, the tune weaving on my internal sheet music to where I knew that I'd be able to complete the entire piece when I sat down. It was thrilling.

But everything came to a screeching halt when I got to my floor. At my door stood none other than Eddie. I thought he had taken the hint, but he had always been a stubborn ass and I should have known better.

Eddie walked toward me before my foot settled on the second-floor landing, his heavy steps booming in the empty hall. He had a menacing glare, and I was fearful of him for the first time.

"Eddie. . ." I said hesitantly.

"Where the fuck have you been?" he asked; his angry voice sent chills down my spine and I visibly shook beneath my jacket.

My feet were frozen in place, and as he got closer, he reached out to grip my arm.

"I asked you a question."

I felt like a catfish. My mouth opened and closed because I was at a loss of words on how to diffuse the situation.

Suddenly an arm wrapped around my waist and hoisted me against a warm hard body. I didn't even care who it was so long as they got me away from my ex. Thankfully I knew after a second that it was Rylan and my body sank against his. He smelled the same as he had in the hotel room, something masculine, clean, and all him.

"Hey, baby. I'm sorry I'm late." He kissed the top of my head before holding out a hand to my visitor. "I don't think we've met. I'm Rylan, Haley's boyfriend."

Eddie sneered at Rylan like he was yesterday's trash and didn't acknowledge the greeting.

"So, this is why you've been ignoring me? Playing around with the campus playboy?"

"It doesn't matter what I've been doing because it's none of your business. We broke up six months ago when I found out you screwed all the chicks in your dorm."

"Why does it matter? He'll screw anything that moves and probably some that don't."

Rylan tensed and I felt him move from behind me. In a flash, he had Eddie pressed against the dingy hallway wall; his forearm held Eddie up by the neck. After the scuffle Eddie would probably send his jacket out for dry-cleaning to remove anything he would have come in contact with.

"Listen here, asshole. You know nothing about me, and obviously, she can do better than you. If you let her go, that's your problem, not hers. Now, you will leave Haley alone and we won't have a problem or I'll make sure you regret it."

Gasping for air, Eddie had the nerve to ask Rylan if he knew who his father was. His father was a local judge of some sort. He threw out the line on more than one occasion when I'd gone out with him.

"I don't fucking care if your father is the President. I'll make sure your body is never found. Now go before I change my mind."

Eddie sank to the ground as Rylan stepped back. I immediately grabbed Rylan's arm, my hands wrapping around it protectively, as if he needed my security. Eddie looked back and forth between the two of us and pushed up from the ground before heading down the steps. I didn't know what conclusion he came to, but I hoped it meant he finally understood that we were over.

"Did he hurt you, Haley?" Rylan sighed beside me, his stare pinned to the wall where he held Eddie.

"No, he never. . ." I started, but I never got to finish what I was saying because Rylan quickly tugged at my hand and dragged me down to my apartment door.

"Open it," he commanded in a voice I didn't recognize — one filled with restraint like he was holding on by a delicate thread.

I dug my hand through my bag until I found the keys, but my hand shook as I tried to insert it into the lock. Finally, I was able to twist the knob and let us inside.

There was no moment of placing my things on the small console table I kept in the entryway. Rylan yanked my bag over my head and threw it in the corner, then cupped my jaw in his hands. He pressed his mouth against mine and it was as if the last five minutes never existed. I was immediately lost in the sensations of his kiss. It was hungry, warm, minty, and familiar all rolled into one.

"Take off your jacket and shoes," he whispered against my lips before he greedily nipped at them.

It was no easy feat to slip off my puffy jacket while he held my face in his palms, but I was thankful I had worn my slip-ons because I easily kicked them across the room.

"Wrap your legs around me," he commanded as he turned and pressed my back against the wall, his erection coming in contact with the place I wanted him most. Images of that night together flickered through my mind and I felt a flood of desire wash over me.

Rylan pulled his mouth away as he discarded his jacket, then wrapped his hands around my thighs as he guided me toward my bedroom. He hadn't been in the apartment since Jolee lived here, but he smartly assumed the one at the end of the hall was mine.

With each step he took my body bounced against his and I felt myself already inching toward an orgasm.

"Rylan," I mumbled against his mouth, my body feeling feverish with need. Had my room turned into a sauna?

Haphazardly he dropped me on the bed and I was thankful that I had made it this morning because I usually got in a fight with my blankets while I slept and they always ended up on the floor.

"Take off your shirt, cat."

I stared up at his glazed-over eyes and knew that this moment wasn't the time to ask about the nickname. Instead, I sat up on the bed and thrust my chest forward, waiting for his eyes to drop to the part of me I tried so hard to disguise, but they remained glued to my own eyes. It was. . .refreshing.

With what little sex appeal I could muster, I grabbed the hem of the black sweater and lifted it over my head. I tried my hardest to suck in my stomach as I lifted, but I was terrible at multi-tasking and let the muscles free as I yanked the sweater over my head. He had seen me naked before in the darkness of my hotel room, so I knew that he was aware of the extra pounds that no gym time would ever help remove.

But I almost gasped at how his stare had morphed from predatory to one filled with wonderment. It reminded me of a kid on Christmas. His eyes glistened as I reached behind my back and unhooked my bra, letting the straps slide down my arms until the black lace rested on my thighs.

"My God, you're the most beautiful thing I've ever seen," he said; his words were breathy as he reached behind his head and tugged his shirt off his body.

Rylan was all hard lines and taut flesh. There wasn't a part of him that wasn't utter perfection and I knew firsthand that his manhood was the most impressive one I had seen. And though I was a newbie to the sex act, I wasn't completely naïve to the average penis size. If he thought I was beautiful, then he was a freaking Adonis begging to be carved into marble.

"Keep looking at me like that and this will be over before it got started," he growled.

Despite the serious nature, I couldn't help but giggle. "You started it."

Stalking toward me, Rylan said, "I'll be sure to finish it too."

He leaned over me and sealed his lips against mine. This time, the kiss was different from any of the others we had shared. It was soft, tentative, explorative, and completely disarming. With just the press of his lips, I was lost to him.

"Lay back," he said as he placed his knee on the bed, the mattress squeaking with the weight shift.

"Rylan," I whispered as he tucked one of his arms under my back and lifted me farther onto the bed as if I weighed no more than a feather.

"Yes, cat?" His lips pressed against the skin along my collarbone — his deft tongue traced the ridge of the bone beneath. Quivers racked my body at the sensation as if I had been electrocuted.

"Is this different than last time? Are we going to go back to hating each other afterward?"

I thought he would hesitate or pull away, but Rylan gazed up at me beneath his obscenely long dark lashes and pressed a kiss to the top of my breast, then another, and another until his lips met the peak of my nipple.

"So fucking different," he added before his tongue laved the tight point. My body squirmed beneath him. No one paid this much attention to my breasts in the way that Rylan was. Every kiss felt like a searing brand on my skin, but the kind that left you begging for more — sadist tendencies.

The arm tucked under me gripped me tight as he continued exploring, switching between my two breasts until I begged him to make me come.

"Please, Rylan. I need more."

"I'm going to fuck your tits one day, cat. I fucking love them."

"Well, I hate them."

"Blasphemy. I'll make sure they get the love they deserve. Now, tell me, where is it you need me?"

I raised my hips so that he could feel the heat coming from my center because I was on fire between my legs, a raging inferno, but he shook his head, those dark strands of hair brushing against his forehead with the movement.

"You need to use your words, cat. I want to hear you say what you want."

"I can't, Rylan." The words I wanted to use were foreign to me, things that my previous boyfriends or dates always tried to suppress and now I was embarrassed to ask for what I wanted most.

Rylan moved up my body until our faces were inches apart at my hesitation. He gently stroked the skin on my cheek, his touch instantly putting me at ease.

"You don't need to feel embarrassed with me, Haley. Tell me what you want, even if you aren't sure, and I will do my best to make you feel good. Okay?"

"Okay, I'll try," I whispered in return. He pressed a soft kiss on my nose and then made his way back down my body until his hands rested on the waistband of my pants.

"Good girl. Now, how do you feel about butt plugs?"

My body jerked up in surprise at his question and I caught his salacious grin. I wasn't sure if he was joking, but the more I thought about the adventures Rylan could take me on, I was less concerned with what anyone else thought. He was already changing me in just a few short minutes.

"I may be up for it eventually."

His eyes widened as he stared up at me. I'd surprised him almost as much as I surprised myself. The soft breaths expelling from his nose brushed across my stomach's sensitive skin, and I clenched the muscles at the feeling.

"Fuck. Am I breathing?"

A chortle escaped as I replied, "Yeah, I think so. Is fuck your favorite word?"

"Fuck yes. Now, stop distracting me, cat. I have business to attend to," he said as he unbuttoned my pants and tugged them down my legs. I secretly patted myself on the back for remembering to shave my legs in the shower this morning.

"And what's that exactly?"

"You have a pussy that I want to become well acquainted with. Lift your hips."

I watched in fascination as Rylan slipped my lace panties down my legs and kneeled back onto his heels as he stared at my naked body. Fear of rejection began to bleed down my spine and the need to cover up became overwhelming. I was that shy pre-teen again everyone was staring at. I moved my arm to cover my chest but Rylan gently grasped my wrist and pulled my arm back down to my side.

"Sorry, I just need another minute to take you in. You're perfection, Haley. There is no other way to describe it."

The insecure girl in me wanted to call him a liar, but the woman in me knew that he was speaking the truth. I'd never had anyone look at me like Rylan was, like I was the ultimate treasure.

"Rylan, I want to come with your tongue between my legs," I requested, breaking the spell.

"Fuck yes. That's my girl," he responded. He dove between my thighs as if it were his last meal.

No one had ever taken the time to explore that part of me. Eddie hated cunnilingus, as he called it, and said it was degrading to him. But Rylan feasted on my sex like it was a freaking honor to be asked. And I wasn't complaining a bit.

I had no idea that it could feel this way. I thought I saw stars when he swirled his thumb around my sensitive clit and inserted a finger deep in my channel while he pressed kisses against my folds. A literal galaxy exploded behind my lids. The light was so blinding I was afraid I'd lost all sight. But as I pried my lids apart, I found a smug Rylan pressing a kiss to my inner thigh.

"My God. Is that what everyone was talking about? I had no idea!"

"Baby, your pussy's so fucking delicious you can ride my face any time you want."

There was no stopping the heat that rose from my chest up to my cheeks, leaving a red stain along my skin, not to mention the instant pool of heat between my legs. Rylan had no idea how is dirty words were affecting me.

"Rylan?"

"Yeah?"

"It's your turn to take your pants off. I want to feel your cock in my mouth."

CHAPTER SIX
RYLAN

I died

There is no other explanation for what happened the moment Haley wiggled her delectable ass out from under me, yanked my pants down to my ankles, and placed her lips on my shaft. It was the sweetest, most delicate kiss I'd ever had on the sensitive skin, and I couldn't get enough.

"Shit. If this is a dream, don't ever wake me up."

Haley giggled as she descended her open mouth on my mushroom head and I felt the vibration all the way to the tips of my toes. Her tongue did this swirl thing where it dipped just inside the hole at the tip and then flattened along the thick vein on the underside. I don't know where she learned that trick but it would be my undoing. If this girl wasn't going to be the death of me, then I wanted to be labeled an immortal.

"If you keep doing that, cat, I'm going to come."

"Mmhmm," she murmured and I almost fell to my knees at the sensations as they vibrated across my skin. Luckily I was able to catch myself on the edge of her bed before I toppled over, probably taking her with me. My fist immediately gripped the bedding as the orgasm came swiftly. A roar escaped from my lungs as I filled her mouth with my cum. It felt like it went on forever.

When I came to, I looked down to find Haley sitting back on her heels, wiping my excess cum from the corners of her mouth. Just the motion of her putting that finger back inside her mouth, savoring what was left of my load, had me almost orgasming again.

"Get your sexy ass on that bed right now."

She eyed me with surprise as she stood. "So soon? Doesn't it usually take a little while?"

"Yes, normally. But not with you. Fuck, can't you see he's standing at fucking attention?"

Her gaze jerked down for a second and her shoulders stiffened and then relaxed.

"We can go slow," I tried to reassure her.

Haley. My cat. The sweet little minx placed her hand on my chest and pushed me until I fell backward onto the bed. Damn, she was full of surprises.

"I want you to show me how you fuck, Rylan. I want to know if the rumors are true."

It felt almost dirty to be here with her like this, knowing she knew of the women that had been in her same place. There was no way she could know how her words hurt or how I wished that my reputation never touched her.

I placed my hands on her hips as she straddled me, the warmth between her legs settled on my stomach.

"I can't do that, Haley."

"Why not?" she asked, her eyebrows rose in surprise.

"Because you're different. You're nothing like any other woman. You're. . .you."

"I don't know why that got me so hot."

"Well, let's think about it later because I want to feel you squeezing my shaft. Condoms?" I asked as Haley began rocking her pussy against my erection. She nodded toward her nightstand and I reached over to grab the unopened box. Fuck, her heat was already driving me wild.

It would be so easy to slide inside her right now, but I knew better than that. But apparently, my cock didn't get the memo because as I worked the condom out of the wrapper, it nudged just inside her entrance. She slid down until I was about halfway in and then stopped, gazing at me with wide eyes.

"Oh fuck. Shit, Haley. I need to get this on," I exclaimed as I reached out with my other hand and gripped her ass, forcing her up and away from my penis.

"Rylan," she moaned.

I worked the condom over my stiffness and aligned the tip at her opening.

"Take what you want, cat. I'm yours."

She tossed her head back as she sank down on my cock, her thighs quivering with each inch that sank deep inside her warmth.

As she filled herself to the hilt, I closed my eyes and groaned her name. It was too much and not enough at the same time.

"I need you to move, cat. For the love of everything on this planet, please move." My body was on a tightly woven thread, ready to snap at any moment. I needed to feel her inner walls stroking me, caressing my delicate skin.

She slowly rose on her knees and then just as slowly lowered herself. Over and over at an agonizingly measured pace. Her hips rocked and as she found her tempo, she reached forward and placed her hands on my chest. She played every inch of my body as if it were music that only she could hear. The rhythm she set had its own beat. Quick, quick, quick, slow, slow.

Our sex was a dance and fuck if it wasn't phenomenal.

"I can't get there, Rylan," she moaned, rocking against me.

"I got you."

Reaching out, I gripped her hips hard enough that I'd probably leave a mark but I couldn't care about that as I held her in place and began thrusting my cock into her channel at a rapid pace.

"Oh. Yes. Right there," Haley cried out as she tilted forward, allowing the tip of my dick to rub her G-spot and clit simultaneously. "I'm coming!"

Her screams reverberated off the walls, and if she'd had pictures hanging, I'd be worried that they'd fall.

As she came down from her high, I flipped us over, pressed my lips against hers, and slowly slid back inside her core.

I knew that she would be sensitive after her release, and I wanted to take my time, but she reached out and dug her fingers in my ass, tugging me harder against her.

"Tell me if it's too much," I explained and waited for her to nod before shifting my weight onto one arm and using my other hand to wrap around her neck and jawline. Her eyes widened at first, and I considered pulling my hand away, but then as I rocked my hips a few times, her breathy moan was the only response I needed.

My thrusts quickened until the sounds of our skin slapping together were louder than our breaths.

"You're so fucking sexy like this. God damn, Haley, I can already feel your pussy clenching around my cock. You like me holding you like this? Wrapping my hand around your neck as I pound into you? Fucking, dirty girl," I growled in her ear, feeling her sex grow wetter.

A moan slipped passed her lips as she bent her legs and brought her knees against my chest. The change in angle had me ready to explode in seconds.

"I'm going to come, Haley," I told her as I went harder with each pounding. My grip tightened against her jaw and I checked her eyes to make sure that she was okay before I tilted my head back and let my release take me over.

Time stood still as I spilled inside the condom. Sex had never been like that for me - explosive, fiery, and perfect. Just like the last time Haley and I were together.

When I could catch my breath, I slid out of her tight sex and rolled over on the bed, making sure to tug Haley's body across mine.

"I think I died." I chuckled with what little energy I had left.

"What a way to go though."

"Agree." I used two fingers to tilt her chin upward. "Are you sure that you're okay? I know not everyone can handle what we just did, but I couldn't hold back."

Haley twisted her body so that she was lying on top of mine. "I'm fine. And I more than liked it. Maybe we could do it again sometime."

Usually when a woman brought up the prospect of a repeat performance, I would shut down and begin gathering my things, but I didn't feel the sudden need to escape with Haley. That should have been a red flag for me, but I was already growing addicted to Haley.

"Fuck yes, we will."

"I think your obsession with that word is out of control."

"I can't help that I like the word fuck and I like *to* fuck. You."

"Flatterer."

There was a peacefulness in the silence that followed. I stroked her hair with my hand, twisting the strands like I had witnessed her do before. It was soft and silky against my rough hands, like sheets at an expensive resort. Her delicate fingers traced the ridges of the muscles along my chest and abdomen. It was comforting. Something I hadn't felt. . .ever.

"Let me toss the condom and then we can grab some dinner?" I asked her, and I wondered if I would be turned down for the first time. "If you want, that is." It's not like sex and coming to her rescue with her ex would change whatever dynamic we'd had.

"Chinese sound good? Or did you want to go out?"

"Maybe we can stay in and watch a movie and have a repeat."

"I like the way you think. I'll go grab the menu."

My muscles ached as I got up to dispose of the condom and I couldn't help but watch Haley saunter out of the room, my eyes lingering on her heart-shaped ass. I wanted to sink my teeth in it.

We ordered a couple of items off the menu and decided to watch the original *Jurassic Park.* It was still daylight outside and the sun cast a mix of light and shadows on the hardwood floor between the apartment issued vertical blinds that hung in front of her balcony doors. They lay on the ground in harmony, one complementing the other. When one moved, so did the other. It was nature's dance. The illusion made me think of Haley and me. Whatever we were was a fantasy because I was nothing more than a broken man that had zero hope of giving any part of me in a relationship.

I had tugged on my boxers, but Haley was naked beneath a blanket while we sat on the couch waiting for our food delivery.

"Haley," I said, drawing her attention away from the movie. We needed to address something that happened, the elephant in the room. "I'm clean. You know since. . ."

She twisted her head to look at me, those dark wavy locks spilling over her shoulder and I wanted to sink my hand into them again. I always liked things that were too good for me.

"I am too."

Silence passed as we gazed at each other. I broke it by whispering her name again.

"Yeah?"

"You. . .um. . .know that this can't be more than sex, right? I mean. I'm not boyfriend material."

"I know. I'm under no false pretenses of what this was. It's just sex. It's really good sex that we should continue with, but I get it. I'm super busy with graduation looming and figuring out what I want to do. I'm sure it's the same for you."

My body relaxed, but it was just a façade because my heart ached knowing that she didn't expect me to stick around. I had never stuck around for anyone, just Mom.

"Yeah, it's the same. And I agree, we definitely should keep fucking."

One of her perfect eyebrows arched high on her forehead and those gorgeous purple eyes stared at me. "Exclusively. I may be new to this no-strings game, but I don't share, Rylan."

"I agree." Under the blanket, my fingers scraped along her knee as she opened her legs up for me. "Maybe we can get started now, cat."

Just as my hands met the warm apex of her thighs, the doorbell rang. We groaned as I got off the couch and grabbed the food, placing it on the kitchen counter.

Shamelessly, I tucked my thumbs into my boxers' waistband and slid them down my thighs until they fell at my feet. I walked behind the couch until Haley was in front of me. She must have sensed my closeness because the pace of her breathing changed. Reaching out, I set my hands on her shoulders and glided them down slowly until they cupped her fantastic breasts. If she was self-conscious of them, she had no reason to be. They were perfect.

Haley tilted her head as I pressed a kiss to the top of her bare shoulder, then her neck, then her jaw. I left a path of pecks until I reached her ear.

"I bet I could make you come just like this, with my fingers playing and pulling at your rosy nipples. They remind me of pale pink rosebuds in the early morning."

"Mmhmm," she mumbled as she lifted one arm until it wrapped behind my head, her hand delving into my hair.

I left one hand on her breast and skimmed my fingers of the other down her stomach and under the blanket until I came to the treasure between her legs.

"Or what if I fucked you with my fingers and rubbed your clit with my thumb until you begged me to let you come."

She moaned, "Yes."

Teasingly I slid my hand up and down on her slit, letting my finger almost slip into her warm sheath but never going inside. The heel of my hand pressed against her bundle of nerves but only made small motions.

"Rylan, please," Haley whimpered.

I teased her a bit longer before I finally succumbed and slipped two digits in her channel; the walls immediately tightened around me. My girl was already close to her release and I loved the power I held over it.

"Don't come, cat. I want to be inside you when you come."

"I. . .I can't stop. . ." she said as she began to rock her hips. She was close, too close.

Regretfully I pulled my hands away despite her protests.

"Touch yourself, Haley. Keep yourself going."

I took a step back from the couch. She eyed me suspiciously but placed her hand where mine had been, her body jerked at the contact, then softened as she began to finger fuck herself. When I could see that she had found her rhythm, I dashed to the bedroom, my hard cock standing at attention as I ran, I grabbed the box of condoms and went back to join her.

The perfectly pale skin of Haley's was now awash with a pink tinge as she worked herself over. With the condom in place, I moved in front of Haley, tugged her by the ankles until her back rested on the armrest, and then flipped her over. Her delicious ass was lifted in the air and I couldn't resist the urge to smack it as I guided my erection into her sex.

She had propped herself up on her elbows, rocking back with each thrust. I knew she was sore, but she met me pound for pound. And I almost came when she twisted her head to glance over her shoulder to watch me. I loved seeing her let go with me.

"I'm so close," she cried out. I reached forward and grabbed her jaw under her chin. She lifted so that my hold kept her upper body in place.

"Coming!" Haley shouted as she reached out for the back of the couch, her hand fisting the cushion.

As her walls squeezed my cock, I followed behind her, spilling myself into the condom.

We both fell forward onto the couch, our heavy breaths in sync as we tried to come down from the high. Pulling my shaft free from her pussy, I pressed a kiss to the middle of her back then stood.

"We should probably eat. To keep our stamina up and all."

She didn't move from her spot on the couch as she replied, "You're probably right."

I walked into the kitchen to discard the condom in the trash and came back out to find that Haley hadn't moved. The corner of my mouth lifted in a smirk as I walked toward her. A slap echoed in the apartment as my palm connected with one of her perfect globes.

"Come on, lazybones. Let's get some food in you."

***

The deal with Haley was going better than I had imagined. We pretty much agreed on a no-strings, all-sex policy. We were friendly but didn't make much effort outside of class to get together unless it was for a roll in the sheets. We were insatiable, fucking at a minimum of two times a day. And I was quickly learning that sex with my neighbor was addictive.

She'd even gone as far as finding the secret room in the library that Keeley and Chance had found last semester. I didn't want to think about my brother screwing his girlfriend in the same space, but when Haley and I scheduled our philosophy study group in the library, we made use of the room. I found that we could only last an hour max in each other's company before we were pawing at each other.

We were leaving philosophy class and I watched as Haley spoke with another classmate as they left. He was tall and muscular, probably an athlete because he reminded me of my brother Tyler, and he definitely had eyes for Haley. I kept trying to tell her that men thought she was gorgeous, but she would shrug her shoulders and brush it off.

The jealousy that surged through me was alarming. I followed at a distance, not because I was snooping but because I wanted to make sure my cat was safe.

Usually, we left philosophy together because she would head to her arts building and I'd go to my last business class of the day, both in the same direction. But Haley hadn't been speaking to me since this morning.

After I woke up with her mouth on my dick, I might add the best way to wake up; she asked if I wanted to go with her to meet her dad for dinner on Saturday night. My worst fears started climbing up my spine, and before I knew it, I had my pants on and I was out her door.

I had messaged her later that morning, reminding her that I didn't do relationship stuff. And she replied that it was just dinner. All I had to say was no thanks.

God, I was just a fuck up. I had reasons why I didn't get close to people. Deep-seated abandonment problems that were the basis of all of my choices. My parents, or whatever they would be called, made sure that they left a smudge on whatever decisions I made in life.

Because what kid likes to be told that their parents disappeared on purpose, and left you in the hospital. Oh, and that there was no record of your birth. That's what every nine-year-old liked to hear. And that was just the first layer of the hell that I lived in.

But Haley was right. It was just dinner and I was making a bigger deal out of it than it needed to be.

Watching her smile up at the jock was the last straw. I stalked over to them, Haley catching sight of me first, and I might have enjoyed seeing her spine straighten as I approached. Swinging my arm over her shoulder, I pressed a kiss to the top of her head.

"Hey, cat. Are you going to introduce me to your friend?"

With a sigh, Haley introduced me to Matt, who didn't miss a beat in shaking my hand. It was evident to anyone that I had staked a claim on this beautiful girl, even if it was just a physical title.

"I need to head to class. Walk with me?" I asked her, hoping that she would take the hint. Luckily Haley said goodbye to the guy trying to get in her pants and agreed to walk with me. When we turned to head toward the business building, she slipped from under my arm and kept at least a foot of distance between us.

"That was rude," she huffed, a puff of air coming out between her lips like a steam engine as she crossed her arms against her chest.

"You're right. It was, but I'm not sorry. We said exclusive."

"You're an asshole. You know that?"

"So you've told me before. That guy wanted to get between your legs anyway. I was saving you."

"Saving me?" She stopped and faced me on the sidewalk, causing other students to have to move around us. "He didn't want between my legs. What he wanted was to see if I could email him a copy of the midterm study guide because he never got the original and the professor won't send it again."

"I like you all fired up." And it was true. I loved when her purple eyes flared. "Has anyone ever told you that you look like a young Elizabeth Taylor?"

"No, and stop changing the subject. You need to stop being a dick to everyone."

"That's where I got your nickname, by the way. You look like her in *Cat on a Hot Tin Roof*. Just in case you were still wondering."

She paused for a moment and stared at me wide-eyed. "Really? That's. . .well. . ."

During her momentary lapse in brain function, I added, "I want to join you tomorrow for dinner. If I'm still invited. I didn't mean to freak out this morning. It just caught me off guard and I have. . .issues with family things."

"Yeah, okay," she sighed deeply. "Can we talk about that later? Your issues?"

The bitter cold swirled around us, winter making her presence known as we stood there on the campus sidewalk. I had a choice to make and I wasn't sure which was the right one.

"Maybe?" I told her because I wasn't ready to decide.

"Alright, well, I have dinner plans with Jolee and the girls so they won't be at your brother dinner tonight. You're hosting, right?"

My brothers and I made it a point to have dinner together every Friday if we could. We rotated cooking and cleaning duties and tonight was my night.

"Okay. Well, I'll just text you in the morning with the time for dinner."

"You're not coming after?"

"I mean. I wasn't planning on it. I figured your brothers would-" I cut her off. Stepping forward, I placed my hands on either side of her head and sealed our mouths together. My tongue dove into her mouth, swirling around her own.

Pulling back only an inch or two, I told her, "I want you in my bed, cat. I can't sleep unless you've come on my dick. Got it?"

I didn't care that some students just witnessed me kissing Haley in the quad, or that this probably changed our relationship status, made our fling public. So long as the males on campus knew they couldn't lay a hand on her, I was fine.

"Yeah. I got it. I'll see you later tonight then. And, thank you, for the compliment. I love Elizabeth Taylor."

I thought she'd slip out of my grasp and sway her curvy hips as she walked back to her apartment, knowing that it drove me crazy. But Haley lifted on her toes and pressed her lips against mine in a chaste kiss. Damn, I loved when that girl surprised me.

I watched her walk away before heading toward the business department building, where a couple of the guys that went on the study abroad program with me chatted outside.

"Saw you with that weird music girl," one of them called out as I walked passed them. I tried to stay on friendly terms with them when we were overseas because they were the only people we'd had for six months. And two of them were decent enough guys, people I would consider friends, but the rest were slimy assholes that needed to be taught a lesson at some point. Daddy couldn't open all of the doors for them or hide all of their secrets.

Ignoring his comment, I continued up the steps, but I wasn't out of earshot yet and heard him holler, "Did you tell her yet? Or are you still stringing her along?"

CHAPTER SEVEN
HALEY

The bar in town, RJ's, was filled to the brim when I made my way inside. I was surprised the girls had chosen the spot for our girls' night, but as I noticed the hockey team taking up the booths on one side of the bar, I realized why. The team had won tonight and drinks were half off. Not to mention the team was just so damn attractive that it was no chore to look at them.

I still believed that the Ridge Rogues were hotter. As did most of the females at Wellington. I don't think the hockey players minded, though.

It took a second passing over the bar to find Jolee, Sarah, and Keeley huddled in a booth in the far corner, close to the jukebox.

"Hey, guys," I said as I skipped over.

The table was covered in appetizers at various stages of being eaten and there was a pitcher filled with a slushy pink liquid. I assumed it was a daiquiri. I was more of a beer drinker myself.

"Haley!" they shouted as I slipped off my jacket and sweater, revealing a black lace bralette I wore as a crop top. That was the one thing about poorly lit bars. No one knew that it wasn't a shirt. Beads of sweat began pooling at the base of my neck under my thick hair when I stepped inside the bar, most likely from all of the bodies in the space, so I was glad to have something light underneath.

"You look freaking hot," Jolee said as I slid across the bench beside Keeley.

I felt hot. Sex with Rylan had pushed my self-conscious tendencies to the back burner. He spent so much time complimenting my body that I was beginning to believe him.

My friends looked equally gorgeous. Sarah was wearing a blue dress that flattered her dancer's body. Keeley must have come straight from her classroom, where she was a student-teacher. She wore a white silk shirt and pencil skirt. The stunner Jolee looked every bit like a runway model in her tight jeans and red leather top, but she had just a hint of dirt smudging her hands from her hard work with the animal shelter.

From beside me, Keeley's eyes narrowed in my direction, which prompted Jolee and Sarah to do the same. Their heads tilted from side to side, examining me.

"What?" I asked, suddenly worried that my lipstick had trailed up and over my lip, but the label assured me it was smudge-proof.

Keeley gasped for air out of nowhere. I would have been worried that she was choking if she hadn't said, "You've had sex! Oh my gosh, that's it. You gave away your v-card."

"Who was it?"

"Do we know him?"

The girls started bombarding me with questions that only drew the attention of the hockey players across the way. As a few of them began to approach, Jolee shouted that we were all taken. One of them eyed me like a snake ready to bite, and for a moment, I thought he wouldn't care that I was taken, but then he shrugged and turned back to his friends. I probably should have corrected Jolee and explained that I was still single, but it was easier this way.

My friends stared at me again, urging me to dish out the details, but the waitress saved me when she stopped by the table and asked if I wanted anything. I ordered a burger, fries, and a lager that they kept on draft.

"Can I at least take a sip of my beer before I embarrass myself in front of you all?"

They hesitantly agreed. Their beautiful faces masked their disappointment with well-placed smiles, but were rewarded when the waitress returned with my drink not a minute later. You'd think they'd just won an award with the way their faces lit up.

"Dammit," I said as I took a hefty gulp of the beer, letting the cool liquid quench my surprisingly dry throat.

I knew I was wasting time as I snuck a mozzarella stick from one of the appetizer plates. My friends remained silent the entire time, knowing that it was going to drive me nuts.

It only lasted a second before I plopped my glass on the table. "Fine. I slept with Rylan. And, well, I'm still sleeping with him," I said in a rush. My cheeks felt like they were on fire and I immediately reached for my glass of beer and took another sip.

I waited for the remarks, the degrading comments that he was a playboy or that I wasn't his typical MO. I knew all of that. But when I looked up,

Jolee, Sarah, and Keeley all had pensive looks on their faces.

"I like it. Y'all make a cute couple, in my head at least," Sarah quietly added as she took a sip of her drink.

"Me too," Keeley said.

Jolee was the last to speak up. She was the one I was closest with and had known Rylan the longest, besides me. "This explains so much. The tension, your muse, the smile Rylan's been wearing. He hasn't been riding Ford's ass as much as normal. It makes total sense. He's been eyeing you since he and Ford came to our rescue that night I fell through the coffee table in our apartment."

We chuckled, remembering that drunken night that Jolee realized Ford was her match.

"I don't know about all of that. We're just having fun, though. Nothing serious." I made sure to add that last bit because I knew those girls would have us walking down the aisle in their minds.

"We'll see. Now tell us how it happened. Was he gentle with you?" Jolee questioned.

The lie was on the tip of my tongue, but I knew I couldn't do that to them.

Setting the tone for the last night in Spain, I described the cocktail party and how Rylan had approached me at the bar. We chatted about home and our friends, laughing at the coffee table scenario Jolee had just mentioned. By the end of the night, he went back to my hotel with me, and that was it. I also added how he snuck out in the middle of the night when he found out I was a virgin.

"You didn't tell him?" Sarah gasped.

"Well, I honestly didn't think anything of it. I wasn't even sure he could tell because he kept going. Apparently, he saw the blood afterward and freaked out. He was pretty pissed."

"I can see why."

It surprised me that they were siding with his reaction, but the more time I had to dwell on it, I realized that I should have told him. I couldn't change the past even if I wished I could.

Thankfully my burger arrived with their meals and we ate and chatted about the upcoming year. Jolee was graduating from her master's program and had secured a grant to open a wildlife sanctuary not far from Wellington and Ford was going to help her run it along with Sarah's accounting skills. Jolee and Ford were both business majors like Rylan. I wondered if he considered working with them. We hadn't spoken about our plans after graduation.

Keeley had applied for some open teaching positions in the area and had her heart set on a private school down the street from the University, but a school in New York had reached out to her, showing interest in having her fill a position there. I wasn't sure how Chance felt about that. I couldn't see him leaving his brothers.

The jukebox switched to an old Carrie Underwood song and the girls immediately jumped to their feet. Keeley shoved me out of the booth with a strength I didn't know she possessed. Before I knew it, the girls had me bouncing in the middle of the dance floor regardless of my disdain for country music. But I could appreciate a good beat like anyone else.

We stayed out on the dance floor through a few more songs, ordering new drinks whenever we were thirsty. The girls and I knew better than to drink anything that had been left unattended.

After an hour, a slow song played, and even though Sarah swayed her hips provocatively to the R&B song, we all decided to head back to the booth to rest for a minute. I was also starving and ready for something else to eat. Dancing always wore me out.

Jolee's squeal of excitement brought our attention to the booth where Ford, Archer, and Chance sat waiting. I wasn't sure how they knew where we were and what booth we had occupied, but I had a suspicion that Jolee was the culprit.

Even though we sat in a booth, it was oversized, and the girls filled in next to their boyfriends. It seemed each bench could easily hold four. A masked smile slid into place as I slowly approached the booth. I tried my hardest to tamp down my disappointment.

"Looking for me?" a deep voice said from behind as he wrapped his arms around my waist and tugged me back against him. I was immediately engulfed in Rylan's scent. Even in the room of sweaty bodies, he smelled delicious.

"You wish." I giggled as his fingers slid along a ticklish spot along my stomach.

"Come with me," Rylan demanded as his hand slipped into mine.

The crowd parted as if he were Moses himself and they were the Red Sea. Rylan guided me toward the back of the bar to a dimly lit hallway. I was surprised no one else was back there.

"You look sexy as fuck, cat," Rylan groaned in my ear as he pressed me against the cold brick wall using his body. "This lacy thing shows off your tits just right. I want to suck them right now."

His erection pressed against my waist and I wanted to wrap my legs around him to feel him between my legs. But the sound of laughter brought me back to the moment.

"Rylan," I said as he pressed his lips at the sensitive skin where my shoulder met my neck. I was trying to get his attention, knowing I'd let him screw me in this hall if he continued. "Rylan," I tried again and he finally pulled back, his hooded eyes gazing down at me.

"Yeah?"

"We can't do this here. Someone could walk by."

Rylan took a moment and I wondered if a war waged inside him the way it did within me. I was a second away from throwing my inhibitions to the wind.

"You're right. I saw you standing there and I couldn't help it, cat."

Since he explained the nickname, I'd grown rather fond of it. To the point that my other *cat* clenched every time he said it. And right now, in the middle of the dark back hallway, I felt like I was melting into a hot puddle at his feet.

"You seemed surprised to see me," he added, sincerity laced in his voice.

"I just. . .wasn't sure what to expect."

"Well, if it makes you feel better, all of my brothers are here. Link and Tyler were at the bar. Tyler is DD."

I recalled that Tyler was the youngest of the brothers and not quite twenty-one.

"Come on, let's go join them."

As Rylan snagged my hand and began walking back toward the booth, I yanked him back.

"I told them. The girls, I mean. About us sleeping together."

I paused and waited for him to yell, say that it was over, and claim that I was adding strings to our already complicated relationship. I even braced myself for him to tell me that I was messing with his playboy persona.

But in typical Rylan fashion, he surprised me when he said, "Okay. I told Link and I'm sure the guys will figure it out."

"You're not mad?"

"Why would I be mad? If anything, it means I can feel you up and no one will say anything."

"Well, maybe you could refrain from feeling me up in front of your brothers. I don't want them looking at my chest."

"Why not? It's fucking glorious. But you're right. I don't want to have to kick their asses for seeing what's mine."

I matched his laugh with a giggle and reached up, lacing my hand in his thick locks. Moving onto the tips of my toes, I tugged his head down and brought our lips together in a quick kiss. But that wasn't enough for Rylan. He wrapped one of his strong arms around my waist and held me to him, his tongue begging for entrance between my lips.

He had me hot and ready to feel his shaft slide inside my core within seconds. I may have huffed like a toddler when Rylan set me back on my feet.

"Let's go, cat. The sooner we join them, the sooner we can go home."

***

Sifting through my closet, I tried to find something to wear for tonight's dinner. I saw black, black, and more black. Normally my shade of choice wouldn't bother me, but I wanted to show Rylan that I could clean up nice, be. . .different. Even though with the way he left me in bed an hour ago, he couldn't care less what I wore and preferred me naked at all times.

When we arrived home from the bar around two in the morning Rylan started what he called a fuck-fest. I was going to spend all day tomorrow disinfecting my bathroom, kitchen, and balcony. My sliding glass doors were going to need a good cleaning, too, unless I wanted any guests to see the streaks of my makeup on the glass. The man was greedy and had me in every different position I could think of, and some that I'd never even considered.

Extending my arm, I gathered a handful of hangers and shifted them to the side, my arm muscles protesting at the movement. A dress that I didn't remember having slid into view and I tugged it free from the rod.

It was bright scarlet red. Almost an identical shade to the bottom of those heels girls went crazy over. It was a long-sleeved scoop neck, body-hugging design that would hit mid-thigh. I would have never picked it out for myself but it was the correct size.

My phone pinged on my desk and I walked over, dress in hand, to read the text. It was the group chat with Jolee, Sarah, and Keeley.

Keeley: What are you wearing tonight?

I had mentioned to the girls while we were eating yesterday that I was bringing Rylan with me to my dad's dinner. It took some explaining that Rylan was going because I was afraid to be the third wheel between my father and his new girlfriend.

Laying the dress on the bed, I took a picture and sent it to the group.

Jolee: You're welcome.

Me: What?

Sarah: The dress, you dork.

Me: I don't understand.

Jolee: We snuck that dress into your closet while you were studying abroad. We knew it would be perfect on you. Now you have a place to wear it.

Me: I want to strangle you guys. But, yeah, it's gorg.

Keeley: You'll knock his socks off.

Me: My dad's?

Keeley: Ew. Gross. Rylan's, idiot.

Jolee: Take a pic when you're ready!

I sent a smiley face emoji in the chat and then started getting ready. Dinners with my dad were typically spent at the house he shared with Mom and I'd cook us something. I had a feeling that tonight he was showing off for his girlfriend by taking us to a fancy restaurant in Boston set along the waterside.

I spent some time curling my long hair into soft waves in my bathroom and applying some light makeup. I didn't want to wear too much because the dress was eye-catching enough. Just a few swipes of mascara were all I needed.

Undoing my robe, I tugged on my undergarments, ensuring everything was properly tucked before slipping the dress on. It fit like a glove and skimmed my body as if it were made for me. The neckline showed off the tops of my breasts. Not indecently for dinner with my father, but Rylan would appreciate it.

The weather was still cold, but there was no snow in the forecast. My instinct was to reach for my decade-old Doc Martens. They were my signature shoe. But my eyes fell on the nude pumps I had worn for my spring performance last year. I hated wearing heels, but they would go well with the dress.

Slipping them on my feet, I strutted over to the oversized mirror in the corner of my room and glanced at myself.

Not too shabby.

The five-minute alarm buzzed on my phone and I made quick work of moving my cards and keys into the small vintage Chanel crossbody bag that had been my mother's. I may not have a lot of fashion sense, but my mother sure did. It was also from her that I had a black wool knee-length coat to wear for the occasion.

I placed my bag on the small table in my entryway as I walked through my apartment aimlessly. I was never good at idle time. My heels clomped on the floor with each step and I imagined the people below me were going crazy with the back-and-forth motion.

When I was about to sit on my couch, a knock sounded on my door. Nerves rattled me and my palms grew sweaty like I'd run them through water; I wiped them down the sides of my dress. Why was I so nervous? It wasn't as if this was a date. And Rylan and I had been intimate, so why should I care about what he thought of me in my dress?

Oh God, I hated it. I needed to change.

Turning, I took a step to head down the hall back to my room when another knock sounded on the door.

"Haley, open up. I know you're in there second-guessing everything."

Damn, I hated when he called me out. I really didn't have time to change either.

I made my way to the door with a shaky breath and twisted the knob. Taking a step back, I pulled the door toward me.

"Holy fuck." The whispered words washed over me and I immediately released the knob, hoping to retreat, but Rylan circumvented my plans when his hand grasped my wrist.

"Don't you dare think of changing. You look breathtaking, Haley. My God, I'm not going to be able to go out in public with you."

Anger and confusion finally had my head perking up and I had the chance to take Rylan in. He wore a dark gray jacket and matching pants. The dress shirt was light blue, almost white, sans tie, and it showed off his toned chest. He left me speechless.

"Wow," I whispered as I gestured for him to enter.

He marched by me, his hand casually gliding across my hip as he went. My body shuddered in response.

"If the car wasn't waiting downstairs, I would say fuck dinner and haul you back to your bedroom. It's almost a shame at how good you look because I'm going to be fighting off every male in the restaurant."

"Same goes for you, Rylan. You clean up nice."

"Thanks. Are you ready?"

"I just need my coat." I turned and grabbed the heavy garment from the small closet by the door. Rylan gathered it from my grasp and held it open for me. I appreciated a guy with manners.

"Your ass looks phenomenal, by the way," he added as he held my hair to the side and placed a kiss just below my ear.

Grabbing my bag, I sifted through the contents until I found the keys and signaled for Rylan to go ahead of me. I locked up and we made our way down to the car my dad sent us – a car service that he used for some celebrity clients when they didn't want reporters following them.

The drive into Boston took about an hour. We enjoyed the scenery for the most part and I told him all about growing up in the city.

Rylan was originally from Maryland, or so he thought, but he moved to Boston when he was eight. I could tell he was being vague, but every time I could get him to open up about his past, I felt myself falling for him.

Those strings we had talked about? For me, they were untwining at a rapid speed. But Rylan seemed to close off more.

I just needed to remind myself that he wasn't relationship material. His past was too much a part of him and he let it dictate his life.

Spring break was coming up and neither of us had plans, but Rylan explained that his brothers and Tracy were taking a trip down to Florida. He shrugged his shoulders and changed the subject when I asked why he wasn't going. But his entire body was tense.

If it weren't for him reaching out to hold my hand, I would have thought my questions ruined the night. I needed his strength to keep calm because once the restaurant came into view, I became a bundle of nerves.

"Hey," Rylan said, tugging my hand so that I would look over at him. He leaned closer until his lips brushed against my ear. Just the feel of his skin put me at ease. "If it gets too much, we can leave, okay? Or we can go fuck in one of the bathrooms. I'm up for both. Either way, I get you naked tonight."

A giggle escaped as I shook my head. "Come on, Casanova. Let's meet my dad's girlfriend."

CHAPTER EIGHT
RYLAN

When we entered the restaurant, Haley was so tightly wound that I was afraid she'd snap like a rubber band. The host immediately escorted us toward the back of the restaurant, where small tables overlooked the boats bobbing in the water. The sun had long ago descended, so the city's lights twinkled as reflections in the water.

"Daddy," Haley greeted with affection as she released my hand and hugged her father.

"Good to see you, sweetie."

"Dad, this is Rylan, my friend from school. Rylan, this is my dad, Dr. Daniel Sinclair." I masked my disappointment at Haley's label of our relationship, but that was what we were, friends that fucked. Daniel shook my hand and seemed surprised that I returned his dominant squeeze.

A cough sounded behind him and Daniel quickly apologized and introduced Gina. She had medium-brown skin with sleek hair that hung just past her shoulders, but her sparkling eyes and warm smile immediately put the group at ease.

It didn't take long to realize that whatever fear Haley had of her father's girlfriend was all misplaced. Gina was warm, kind, and a freaking spitfire, like Haley. Apparently, the attorney was a bit of a rock music fan herself and the two women spoke animatedly during the appetizers. I could see on Haley's father's face that it was a relief for him.

"Dr. Sinclair, Haley tells me that you're an orthodontist?" Obviously, Haley had made a new best friend in Daniel's woman, so any hopes of her adding to the conversation were slim to none. She had filled me in on the car ride and I used whatever details she instilled to make conversation with her father.

"I am. I've got a pretty successful practice. Tell me about you. How did you and Haley meet?"

"Oh, we met about two years ago. We live in the same apartment complex and when my brother began dating Haley's roommate, Jolee, we would all hang out."

At the mention of Haley's name, Gina joined the conversation and mentioned that it was great that we had known each other for a while, even though we made sure to insist that we were just friends.

"What are you studying, Rylan?" Gina asked with genuine curiosity in her voice.

"Well. . .I. . .um. . ."

"Rylan is a business major," Haley chimed in. "When we were studying abroad, we did a segment on museums, and I noticed how Rylan connected with the facility director in Italy. Even if he doesn't find something right away, Jolee's wildlife sanctuary will be opening in the fall. Pretty much all of his siblings will be working there, so I'm sure he'd have a spot if he wanted."

"That sounds incredible," Gina added as the server brought out our meals.

My mind was reeling that Haley had paid close attention to how I reacted to the museums. Maybe it was because I had never visited one as a child with my parents. The only time had been to an aquarium with my school on a field trip.

There was something about watching people learn and experience things in an environment outside of a school or home. But it was also what made Jolee's plans so intriguing. I knew Ford and Jolee both had business degrees as well. They most likely didn't need another set of hands, but they might be open to some ideas of how to teach people about the wildlife that would be brought in.

Fuck, I was confused. Haley was the best lay I'd ever had, I was addicted to her, but she was getting too close. I feared I would spill all my dirty secrets, even those that would hurt her. And as I sat here with her family, it made me realize that I needed to end things.

We were growing attached. It was why I had a no-strings rule, but here I was on a date. I was wearing a suit that my mom, Tracy, had helped me find this morning.

Subtly I placed my hand on Haley's thigh under the tablecloth, reveling in her soft skin against my palm. We were getting too deep and we needed to cut ties before it would destroy us both. I already knew that I'd never meet another woman like Haley. No one would ever come close to her. But I promised myself years ago that no relationship was worth the destruction that I could cause. And I would destroy her, even without trying.

Dinner went by agonizingly slow. Or that's how it felt to me. And when we finally got in the car for the ride home, it was well past 10pm. Haley had rehearsal for her spring performance tomorrow morning with the girl who was going to sing her original composition. When she rested her head on my shoulder during the ride home, I didn't have the heart to wake her up to talk about everything.

Instead, I carried a sleeping Haley up the stairs to her apartment. She barely stirred as I sifted through her bag for her keys to unlock the door and continued to carry her to her bed.

"I'm sorry I'm so tired," she said as she sat up and yawned.

She looked adorable with heavy lids and puffy lips, like a beautiful porcelain doll. "Well, all that sex will do it to you. Want help getting out of the dress?" I asked, but she shook her head and explained she needed to use the bathroom.

Removing my jacket, I sat on the edge of her bed and waited for her to come back out. She didn't disappoint as she came back to the bedroom sans clothing and slivered under the covers of her bed.

I wasn't sure how to put into words what I needed to say, but Haley was already starting to drift off, and I knew I needed to make it quick.

"Haley?"

"Hmm?" she replied.

"I think we need to go back to being just friends," I told her, my dick crying in despair, knowing that he'd go without both of his favorite cats.

"Okay."

"Okay?" I was surprised by her response, but maybe she had the same reservations I had. Haley turned over in bed, her back to me as she faced the window.

"Yeah. Can you lock the door on your way out?"

That was it? She wasn't going to fight me or cry and carry on like every other woman when I explained that it was a one-time thing?

As I left her bedroom and closed up her apartment, I couldn't help but think that maybe I had made a colossal mistake.

***

I had been trying to ignore everyone for the last month. My brothers, Haley, and Mom could not get through to me even though they attempted. I wasn't surprised that my brothers and Mom insisted that I fix things with Haley, not that we had anything more than a physical relationship. But the friendly texts from

Haley were a double-edged sword. I craved them even though I never responded.

It was idiotic of me to break whatever commitment we'd had, but I wasn't in the right headspace for her. She needed someone capable of love and that wasn't me.

Spring break was next week. Mom was doing her best to get me to join the crew in Florida, but I couldn't do it.

There were good and bad foster families and I had lucked out when I was brought to Dr. Fincher, who then adopted me. But I had gone through a series of bad ones. The worst was the man that had an affliction for assaulting little boys, me included. He was now living in the southernmost tip of the state that my family planned on visiting.

The chances of ever running into him again were nonexistent, but I couldn't take that chance. I also feared that I would kill him if I ever saw him or his family again. They were the ones that had testified against me and claimed that I was lying. But conclusive test kits were enough to convict him. I was fortunate to have a good social worker on my side. Plus, I was too pretty for prison.

The gym had become my haven. Even when my brothers tried to track me down, it was easy enough to ignore them in the large space. Headphones came in handy.

Upping the incline on the treadmill, I continued my run until a large hand ripped my headphones off.

"Her ex has been snooping again." Fucking Link was nosier than any sorority chick I had ever met. Somehow that man knew everything about everyone.

Stopping the machine, I planted my feet on either side of the running deck.

"So? If she has issues, she'll tell me. She still messages me."

"But you never respond. You couldn't even sit in the same booth the last time we were all at RJ's together."

"What is it you want me to do? Stalk her? Stalk the ex? Put out a hit? Seriously, Link. She can handle herself."

"You're so freaking stubborn; you know that? You're so caught up in your past drama that you can't move forward with something that could make you really happy. That family that abandoned you? They never deserved you, brother. You have the best family here waiting with open arms for you to accept us, but you won't. You push us all away. Well, we're all fucking tired of it.

"Get your head on straight. Talk to someone, anyone, and realize that you can have it all."

"Is that it?" I barked as I snatched my headphones back from him.

"No. Fix that shit with your girl. You both put on a good front, but you're both miserable. It's depressing to watch."

Link finally took the hint and left me on the gym equipment. I started at a jog and worked my way up to the steep incline run that I had begun before I was interrupted. Just mentioning Haley had visions of her flashing behind my eyes. She had been innocent but so free in her lovemaking. Her body writhed like a flame dancing to its own slow melody when we came together. It was intoxicating.

Remembering the night before her father's dinner and how she had moaned as my cock slipped inside her, my feet tripped up on the treadmill and I had to catch myself on the armrests before faceplanting on the belt.

"Fucking hell," I mumbled as I jumped off the equipment.

Chuckles sounded off in the distance and I saw Link hunched over in laughter as he stood by the barbells. Asshole.

I didn't need to make things better with Haley. I needed to forget about her. But it seemed that was easier said than done. Every day that went by without Haley, I grew more anxious to be with her. But I didn't want to give her the false hope of happiness because whatever issues my birth parents had were passed down to me.

The walk back to my apartment was quick because it was freezing outside and I was clad in my gym shorts and tank, but I was eager to check my email. After class, Dr. Caldwell said I should be hearing back about the neurological music therapy internship today. I was hopeful that I was the right fit, but it was hard to get a read on the Director of Operations when we had the video interview.

My eyes flicked down the hall on the second floor as I climbed the stairwell. Subconsciously I looked for Haley everywhere even though I didn't want to. It couldn't be helped. She was in my veins. I felt like a stalker sometimes.

I found Jolee standing by my open apartment door when I got to the third-floor landing. I didn't want to know how she got a key, probably from Link, that bastard.

"Shouldn't you be packing right now?" I asked as I walked passed her into my space, heaving my gym bag into the corner by the laundry room.

"Nope. I finished this morning. Why aren't you packing?" The stubborn woman followed me into my bedroom and sat casually on the edge of my desk as I stripped out of my shirt. If she were anyone else, I'd worry that she was here to try and seduce me, despite my brother, but Jolee was madly in love with Ford, and I thought of her like a sister. I also had a suspicion that my brother was going to make it official with her on the trip.

"Do you mind?" I grunted as I kicked off my shoes and worked at the tie on my basketball shorts.

"I certainly don't." I sneered at her and she rolled her eyes as she stood from the desk. "I'll be in the living room. You have five minutes before your brother bursts in here and accuses you of making moves on me."

She sauntered away and I had no doubts that my brother would do exactly that. He was quite possessive of Jolee.

Their relationship surprised me from the get-go. The two were complete opposites and Ford was a mean bastard when they met. His sole purpose in life was to destroy his birth father, who happened to be the famous Senator from Massachusetts, Senator Rutherford Hastings. It took losing her and the fear of her returning to Alaska to get his head out of his ass.

"I see you're thinking real hard over there."

"Fucking hell, woman. Can't you give a man some privacy?"

"Nope. Look, my guess is it's finally sinking in that maybe you and your brothers are more alike than you thought. All of you have some sort of past emotional. . .let's call them impairments. You struggle with relationships, and love, and intimacy."

"I don't have issues with sex."

"Intimacy, you idiot. None of you have issues with sex if the women of Wellington are to be believed. It's the connection you all struggle with.

"But let me make something very clear. You are capable of more than you see for yourself, Rylan. I don't care if that is with Haley or anyone else. You need to realize that you can give and accept love. You hear me?"

Somehow she'd hit the nail right on the head. I had no idea what love was. I'd never felt its power or witnessed its worth.

Except maybe I had and I never realized it.

"Yeah, I hear you."

"Good. Now, I'll ask again. Are you going to pack?"

"I can't, Jolee. It's. . .there is more to it."

"Is there? Because from where I'm sitting, the only thing standing in the way of enjoying time with the people that love you unconditionally is you."

Releasing my hold on the ties of my shorts, I delved my hands into my overgrown hair that desperately needed a trim.

"Jolee. You don't understand. I. . ."

She stood patiently waiting for my explanation and I knew that I could lie and feed her some excuse, but after the exhausting conversation with Link this morning, I wanted to tell someone. And for some reason, Jolee had always had that impact on us brothers.

But before I could speak up, Jolee reached out and grasped my wrist.

"You don't need to tell me anything, Rylan. The person you need to talk to is living one floor down. But we all have triggers and pasts that shape who we are. Do you want them to continue molding you in the future? Or would you rather take control of your own life?

"Anyway, I'll leave you to it. Flight leaves at 8am."

In the sassy way that only Jolee possessed, she left my bedroom with her words lingering in the space. It was like they were graffitied on the walls in thick black paint; each single droplet of excess was the emotion that they elicited.

Removing the rest of my clothes, I stepped into the shower and rinsed myself off, hoping that the hot water would help me clear my head. It did little. With a towel wrapped around my waist, I wiped the steam from the vanity mirror. The reflection showed the scared boy waiting for someone to take him in, waiting for someone to love him, someone that never even existed.

Stepping into my bedroom, Jolee's words remained, hitting me with every turn. Until finally, I'd had enough. With my towel wrapped around my waist, I reached under my bed and grabbed my small suitcase. It seemed like I was joining them on vacation after all.

There were a few messages I needed to send. First to Jolee for her talk. The second was to Ford for not putting a ring on her finger yet. To which he replied with a picture of an enormous ring in a blue box. My suspicions had been correct. Lastly, I messaged Mom and thanked her for sending Jolee to speak to me. Mom had ways to get what she wanted and a pocket full of secret weapons ready to unleash. Jolee's visit had Mom stamped all over it. She was also thrilled that I had decided to join the family but had understood my hesitancy.

The dresser drawer opened with a squeak and I grabbed a pair of jeans and a shirt, then opened another, encountering the same sound, and took out a pair of boxers and socks.

Dressed, I started throwing warm weather clothes into the open suitcase. Just as I finished zipping it closed, my laptop pinged from my desk with a new email. With Jolee's surprise visit, I had forgotten about the internship email.

Nervously I walked to the device and touched the pad to awaken the screen. I looked up and released a deep breath. This internship meant a lot. Not just to me but to the university as well. I'd heard that I was competing with other Ivy League business majors from Harvard and Yale for the spot.

Before I could second-guess myself I clicked the email and began reading. The subject line in bold letters read: Internship Opportunity. The first three paragraphs were gibberish and repeated everything we had discussed during the interview, but the first sentence of the fourth paragraph was the words: we would be honored to have you as a summer intern.

I knew that I could read the rest later and figure out how to accept, but I had no other thoughts except to tell Haley.

Grabbing my keys, I dashed out of my apartment, the door slamming behind me, and practically jumped down the stairs to her landing on the second floor. My feet couldn't carry me fast enough as I sprinted toward her door.

I pounded incessantly on her door, not even knowing if she was home or not, but my eagerness was well rewarded when Haley answered the door in tight pants and a black t-shirt.

"Rylan?" she asked with a husky voice and I wondered if it was from sex or sleep.

"Sorry, I. . .Fuck, I got the internship, cat."

"I just woke up. Give me a second." At least that answered my question. I was secretly thrilled that she was alone. "Was this the neuro music one?"

"Yes, cat. The one that is the first for the school." Grabbing her hands, I tugged her into a hug, relishing in the smell of her honey-scented hair.

"That's amazing, Rylan. Congratulations." She grinned warmly, genuine happiness radiating from her pores.

"And. . .I decided to join my family on spring break. So, I won't see you for a week."

"Oh, wow. Jolee was able to convince you, huh?"

"You all were in on it?" I asked, surprised.

"No, but Jolee is the most capable of convincing anyone to do anything. She really missed her calling as an undercover agent or something. I also think Ford is going to propose. I'd hate for you to miss that."

"Yeah, he is. Well, I guess I'll. . ." I said, trailing off as I took a step back.

"I'm really proud of you," she added, and fuck if I could control myself. Stepping forward, I cradled her face in my hands and kissed her for everything she was worth.

"I'll see you in a week, okay?" I said, pulling back and left her standing there slack-jawed without a backward glance.

And it damn near killed me.

CHAPTER NINE
HALEY

A week seemed like such a short time to be away from my friends. Was I jealous? Absolutely. They were gallivanting in the Florida sun while I was stuck in Boston with my dad. He'd offered to pay for me to go to New York City for the week to visit my cousin Alexis, but I was fine sitting in my childhood bedroom watching mindless reality television.

It felt surreal to be here whenever I visited. At one point, Dad and I couldn't step foot on the property and were forced to live out of hotel rooms, then our car when the state froze his assets. Mom had done her best to keep us in good spirits, but inside she was blaming herself.

When the trial ended and my dad was named innocent, we were able to move back home, but it took years for his name to shine once again. Mom had struggled the most and took her life in the guesthouse that resided out back. Father refused to demolish it, but we rarely stepped inside, leaving it in the same state Mom would have left it.

There were still so many unknown answers. I was barely a teenager when it all happened, but I never dared to pry my father for more.

A knock sounded on my bedroom door and I called out for them to enter while I shoved another handful of popcorn into my mouth.

"Hey, sweetie."

"Dad!" I exclaimed. "You're home early." It was barely three in the afternoon on a Wednesday, which was typically his busiest day. "Is something wrong?"

"No," he said, but when I arched my eyebrow in his direction, he added, "Well, yes, maybe."

Giggling, I said, "Well, which is it?"

He joined with a chuckle and sat at the edge of my bed. "Nothing is wrong, but I wanted to talk to you."

"Okay," I replied, grabbing the remote and pressing the power button, turning off the television. "What's up?"

"I'm thinking of selling the house. It's just me here, and sometimes you and Gina. But it's too much space for me and I'm rarely home."

My chest ached at the thought of my dad selling the house that Mom claimed had been her dream home. "But Mom. . ."

"I know, sweetie. That's what makes this so hard. She loved this house, but. . .it hurts to be here without her. I see her everywhere, Hales."

"And you can't move on."

"Gina, asked me to move in with her. She'd have a room for you and her place is really nice. It's on the water. But I just. . .the memories keep me anchored here, sweetie."

My dad sounded like he was in agony thinking about leaving, but I understood that we both needed to take this step.

People came in and out of our lives so frequently that you needed to keep them at arm's length if you didn't want to get hurt. There was a reason I was so quick to let Rylan off the hook for needing a break. The step back in our relationship kept me from falling more in love with him than I already was.

I couldn't imagine losing the person you loved the most and having to surround yourself with their things every day. Would I miss coming home to the house where I grew up? The place I learned to ride a bike and came down the stairs in my prom dress? Sure. But there would be new memories and I felt like my dad needed me to be strong and help him with this decision.

"I get it, Dad. I think it's great that you and Gina want to move in together. I like her."

My father blew out a sigh of relief, his shoulders sagging as he exhaled. "You have no idea how much better I feel knowing that you're okay with it."

"Well, I'm not okay. But I will be. This is the only place I've ever known."

"Yeah, but one day you'll have a husband and you will make your own home. How is Rylan, by the way?"

"I told you we're just friends. He's in Florida for spring break."

"That boy didn't look at you like you were just friends. But," he said with his hands in the air, "what does an old man like me know?"

"You're not an old man. You're delusional. And he didn't look at me like anything. Come to think of it; maybe you should get your eyes checked."

"Funny. Want to go out for pizza tonight?"

Memories of pizza parties as a kid flooded my mind and I sat up in bed with a joyful grin on my lips. "Pizza Palace?"

It was as greasy of a pizza joint as you could find in downtown Boston, and I loved it.

"Is there anywhere else?"

"Yes!" I cried out joyfully as my dad stood and walked to my door. "Hey, Dad? Do you think you can tell me more about. . .everything? I think I deserve to know."

The pizza palace was exactly as I remembered. A bit dingy. A bit greasy. And a bit crowded. But the pizza was so freaking delicious that I practically had an orgasm after the first bite. I made a mental note to bring Rylan here but then thought better of it. I wasn't exactly sure what terms we were on. We'd agreed to be friendly, then he left me with that scorching kiss and I was confused again.

Dad and I chatted about school and what my plans were after graduation. I explained that I had applied to a few songwriter fellowships and production companies. Performing wasn't something I was interested in, but I didn't hate it. Then I thought back to Rylan's internship and I wondered if music therapy was something in my field. Under the table, I brought out my phone to send an email to my advisor and asked what options I may have in that field.

When Rylan mentioned the internship option, I'd done some research and found it fascinating, but I never thought about it for myself.

Just as I hit send on the email a text popped up with a picture.

Jolee: HE ASKED! I SAID YES!!!

Holding the phone up, I showed my dad the picture of Jolee's ring. It was a stunner, probably four or so carats. Ford had money in a trust that he refused to use until now, it seemed.

"I think you got a message from someone," my dad pointed out.

Turning the phone back toward me, I saw a text from Rylan.

Rylan: The bastard finally did it. Took long enough. Miss you, cat. Wish you were here.

"Just friends?" my dad asked suspiciously and I replied by shoving a piece of pizza in my mouth.

"So, I think I've stalled enough." From the leather bag my dad carried everywhere, he exposed a sealed manila envelope. "This has everything in it. You can read it now or wait until we get home. I promise I'll answer any questions. And you're right. You deserved to know sooner. I guess I wasn't ready to have this part touch you yet."

Reaching for my glass of water, I sipped the iced liquid through a straw until it slurped at the end. My fingers fumbled with the lip of the envelope until I finally decided that I'd rip it all off like a band-aid. If I wanted to stop and take it home, I knew that my father would oblige.

The stack of papers was larger than I imagined, and I wasn't surprised to see the words, Malpractice, on the header. I was aware of my father being sued, but not for the reason. Senator Hastings' legitimate daughter accused my father of performing sexual acts on her without consent while at his office for a scheduled visit.

I read through the transcription of the trial. It seemed that my father was acquitted after a year due to surveillance equipment at his facility and a requirement that a secondary person remain in the room with patients. But my father's life had been forever changed. Not six months later, my mother committed suicide, blaming herself for the loss of my father's integrity.

Flipping through the pages, my mother's therapist released the documents, per my mother's consent. They stated that Senator Hastings had propositioned her when he had moved into our neighborhood, but she had vehemently turned him down. Hastings moved his family to another community shortly after, but the scorned male had falsified the allegations against my father as his revenge for my mother's denial.

The man should have been put in jail. Everything concerning my mother was swept under the rug because he had his hands in so many jurisdictions.

I sat for twenty minutes reading and re-reading everything until I sat back speechless.

"She was ashamed and it ate at her every day."

"But she did nothing wrong," I cried, tears filling as pools along my lower lashes. The room began to blur like a watercolor painting.

"We know that, but she felt guilty for everything we had gone through."

"I. . .I wish I could kill that bastard," I hissed through my teeth. I was seething at the destruction that man caused. And it pained me even more that Ford and Keeley were his children out of wedlock.

"He's lucky that he died of a heart attack because I know there would be a line a mile long waiting to have their go at him."

"God, Dad. How long have you known about all of this? Doesn't it kill you?"

"Since the day he hit on your mother and followed her to our house, I've known. He even tried to break in, but our neighbor, Mr. Hendrix, stopped him.

"You have to know, sweetie, that your mother already had battles with her demons. She suffered from mild depression and had been taking medication for it that had been working. But this threw her over the edge and she couldn't cope. You can see she tried. God, Haley, she tried so hard to get better after this. Therapy sessions almost twice a day, an uptick in dosage of her meds, but nothing was working. She even considered an inpatient treatment, but it was too late. The day she took her life was when she ran into Hastings' wife at the store and the woman blamed her for everything our family went through. It was too much."

"Gosh. . .I. . .." Tears began falling in earnest, wishing that I had been enough to pull my mom from her depression and the guilt that she felt, wishing that I'd been able to hug her one last time.

"I'm sorry, Haley. Your mother loved you fiercely; she just didn't love herself enough."

"I think. . .I want to go home."

"Of course, sweetie."

The car ride wasn't long, but we sat in silence. Not even the radio on. I felt myself sneering at the house Hastings had once lived in, wondering if the family living there now knew of the awful things that man did.

Our house came into view and Dad guided the vehicle into the driveway stopping just outside the garage.

"Does Gina know?" I quietly asked as I tapped my fingers on the edge of the envelope.

"Maybe some, but I plan to tell her everything if that's okay with you."

I stared up at the house I grew up in and saw everything in a different light. This was no longer what I remembered but instead a building covered in a cobweb of memories.

"Yeah. I'm okay. I like Gina. And I think you should sell the house."

My father sighed in relief, the sound bouncing off the car's interior. "That. . .that makes me happy, Haley. I'll always love your mother, but I. . .I love Gina too."

"I know, Dad. I'll always love her too."

I spent the last few days of spring break packing up the things in my room so my dad didn't need to do it later and we put them in storage. But other than that, I spent most of the time watching reality shows, snacking, or sleeping.

This was a good alternative to being in Florida with my friends.

In my group text with the girls, they made sure to send me daily updates of what they were doing and took pictures on the beach. Jolee made sure to sneak in a daily photo of Rylan in his board shorts tossing a football with Link. God, he was gorgeous. And by the stares of the women in the background, they all thought so too.

It pained me to think that he may be hooking up while on vacation. After all, he was no saint, but I had no claim on him.

Eddie had tried to reach out and see if I wanted to grab lunch while he was in Boston and I ignored his message. It still confused me why he thought I would ever come crawling back to him. Cheating was a big no in my book.

In the morning, I was returning to campus a day early. I missed my apartment and my keyboard. Since learning about my mom and dad, I felt a slow ballad building and I wanted to spend some time working it out. My dad had a piano in the living room that I used to practice on, but it hadn't been tuned since Mom died. He said when he moved, he'd put it in storage for me.

Grabbing my phone, I opened the messaging app.

Me: When are you getting back?

Jolee: Sunday morning. You?

Me: Tomorrow. I have a song to work out.

Keeley: That's great. We should get together Sunday night.

Me: Don't you have dinner with Rogue mom?

Sarah: Rogue mom. Haha. I'm going to start calling her that.

Me: Please don't tell her it was me!

Jolee: I think we can spare one Sunday night.

Me: Dinner here? I'll order Mexican.

Keeley: Yes! No margaritas though. I have class early on Monday.

Me: Deal.

I thought about closing the app, but my finger hovered over the message from Rylan. I hadn't responded, not sure what to say.

Me: Hey. See you in class on Monday.

Rylan: I'll see you b4.

Well shit. What did that mean?

I didn't know what I expected when I arrived at my apartment the next morning. Maybe something life-changing, or one of those surprise décor overhauls that happened when you were away. But all I noticed when I arrived was that everything was a little dusty and I needed to do some laundry.

Dad had seemed both excited and sad when I packed up this morning. It was bittersweet. I was leaving my childhood home for most likely the last time, but Dad and I were moving forward. Gina had come by with donuts and she seemed less cheery than I'd come to know her as I loaded up my car. Normally I rode the train into town or took a car service, but since Dad was packing things up, I decided to bring my little Audi back to campus. I was paying for a parking spot anyway; I might as well use it.

I'd missed my car. She was a high school graduation gift from my mother. It was a small account she had already set aside for that specific purpose. When we picked out the vehicle my dad had mentioned that my mother had been eyeing the same one a few years prior.

Since living in the apartment by myself, I felt lonely for the first time. Usually, I craved the solitude, but after a week of seeing my friends frolic in the ocean, I was a bit crushed.

After unpacking the few items I brought from home, I eyed my keyboard in the living room corner. I had been working on the ballad, but something wasn't working. The harmony didn't meld with the melody, which made it all sound like a big mess. It infuriated me.

Instead of pushing myself to work on the song, I decided to enjoy the courtyard behind the complex. The winter weather in Boston finally gave way to spring and we were enjoying a rare day in the mid-seventies.

Grabbing my notebook, I left my apartment with a skip in my step and made my way outside. The courtyard was large, about half the size of a football field, and there were already a few residents enjoying the space.

A large oak tree beckoned my name and I made my way to a spot in the sun at the base of her trunk but would be shaded once the sun was high in the sky.

Placing my notebook on my lap, I closed my eyes and let the words flow. Writing poetry was the easiest way for me to create lyrics for a song. There was already a beat that flowed with each line and translating it to a different melody only took a bit of tweaking.

By the time noon hit, I had written ten different poems. Some were about a love lost, others about finding yourself, and one I knew for certain had been about Rylan. The words described being denied a childhood, growing up without knowing who you were, and denying yourself love. And maybe unintentionally, it had been about me too. Even though we had very different situations, I'd had those experiences as well.

Glancing down at my bare legs peeking out of my sundress, I noticed they were turning a shade of pink. I couldn't see my shoulders, but I'd probably have some redness there too. I forgot that it wasn't impossible to get sunburnt even in the early days of spring.

Pushing up from the ground, I stood, yawning in the process. Despite having a relaxing break, I was exhausted from all the emotions I went through in the last few days after learning about my mom and the situation that caused her to take her life.

Knowing that Ford and Keeley's birth father was the culprit left me reeling. Could I even look at them tomorrow and not unintentionally hold them accountable for his wrongdoings? I'd like to believe that I could, but I also knew that my emotions were likely to guide me.

As I entered the complex, a message popped through on my phone — an image from Jolee of the entire group at brunch on the beach. The server must have taken it because Jolee was in this image. Everyone looked so happy and I longed for my dad and I to have a family vacation like that. We hadn't taken one since Mom's passing.

Me: Looks fun!

I replied to her.

Bringing up my messages to Dad, I forwarded the picture and added a note.

Me: We should plan a vacation for this summer. Me, you, and Gina.

He quickly responded that he loved that idea and that I needed to start looking for an island somewhere in the Caribbean.

Approaching my floor, I missed the third step from the top, too busy reading my messages, and lost my footing. My knees took the brunt of the impact, but my palms and phone didn't come out unscathed.

"Shit," I cried out. Anti-skid guards covered the stairs because we lived in a snow-prone area and they scratched my knees and hands to pieces. I felt woozy when I looked down and saw blood dripping down my shins. I hadn't thought the fall had been that hard, but I'd been wrong. Blood only bothered me when it was my own.

"Haley?" a voice called out from above me and if I already thought I was having a bad day, this was just the cherry on top.

With as strong of a voice as I could muster, I said, "Eddie, what are you doing here?" As I gingerly stood, I grabbed my phone, which thankfully only had a cracked corner on the screen protector, and glanced at him.

The look of despair on his face actually surprised me. He hadn't even shown that sort of emotion when I told him that we were over for the final time. Of course, he rarely ever believed me when we split up. Eddie was so sure that we'd be walking down the aisle after graduation. Too bad for him, monogamy was a big sticking point for me in a relationship. Not even Rylan had strayed when we were sleeping together. Well, at least to my knowledge.

"Are you okay?" he asked as he held a hand out to assist me, and if my knees didn't hurt so bad, I would have turned him away, but I really did need the help.

"I'll be fine."

"Look, I get that you hate me, but at least let me help you, Haley. You don't have to be alone all of the time."

"Again. What are you doing here?" I persisted as I waited for his answer. I figured Rylan had scared him enough to stay away.

Eddie blushed as he shuffled his feet, seeming embarrassed. "I was on my way to visit someone on the third floor. A girl I've been seeing."

I wasn't sure what to say or what he had expected. A jealous ex? My approval? Frankly, I didn't care.

"So, are you going to stand there bleeding like a stubborn mule or let me help you?"

I began to hobble to my door, ignoring his jab, but it stung all the same. I rarely asked for help, but so few times in my life had anyone been there. Even Mom had been preoccupied a lot when I was a child, which now I knew was most likely due to her depression or medicine. Then after she left us, Dad was in his own world, coping with the loss. I'd grown accustomed to only relying on myself.

Finally, my door was in front of me and I grabbed the key from my bra, it really was the best storage system, and unlocked it. I hesitated before inviting Eddie inside. I wasn't scared of him, but I remembered how he grabbed my arm the last time he came by.

I walked as quickly as my cuts would allow toward my kitchen, grabbed the largest knife I had, and held it by my side as I gestured for him to sit on the couch. I didn't like seeing him there, a spot that Rylan frequently used for our extracurriculars.

"Is there something else, Eddie?" Smartly he eyed the knife in my hand and visibly swallowed.

"Is that necessary?"

"With the way you acted last time, yes, I think it's necessary." I made sure to ignore the boyfriend part.

"Well, now that I'm here I should apologize to you. For my actions last time that I saw you and for all the times I was with someone else."

"Thank you. Your apology wasn't needed, but I appreciate it."

Turning away from me, Eddie leaned forward, placed his elbows on his knees and tilted his head toward the floor. Quietly he said, "You know, a part of me is glad that you found out. I hated lying to you and sneaking around, but I knew you weren't happy with me."

"I don't really want to have this conversation with you." My knees and palms were aching, but he was making my chest ache too. Those years were lost to a boy that never actually cared about me.

"I know. I just wanted to get it off my chest. It was never you. You're perfect. It was my hang-up."

Silence filled the room. I wasn't sure how he wanted me to respond. He didn't need my forgiveness to move on. My guess was, with graduation looming, the thought of life after college hit him hard. It tended to do that to seniors.

"Thank you for saying that. I need to finish unpacking."

Wordlessly he stood and walked to the door, his brown leather loafers shuffling against the hardwood floors. I'd never made it a secret that the noise irritated me. I'd always hated how he never picked up his feet as he walked. He must have noticed my cringe as he reached the door.

"See you around, Haley."

"Bye, Eddie."

When the door clicked shut, I placed the knife on the counter and carefully limped to the door and locked it before heading back to my room. I needed to get this mess on my legs cleaned up; the blood had already reached my ankles.

God, I was a mess. These cuts would make wearing pants for the next few days a nightmare. Putting my phone on my bed, I stared down at the palms of my hands. These were no better and writing was going to be a bitch. It seemed like I was going to need to use a voice recorder for classes next week.

I'd already showered this morning, but I knew another would be the easiest way to clean this mess up. The hot water stung and I lied to myself claiming the tears were just water splashing on my face.

By the time I got out of the water, I was completely exhausted and hurting. The first aid kit under my sink came in handy as I spread the antibiotic ointment over the cuts on my knees and hands. I filled the cup on the counter with water and popped two acetaminophens in my mouth, swallowing them with the water to numb the pain.

After drying off, I walked to my dresser and grabbed a pair of panties and an oversized Avenged Sevenfold shirt that I snagged from Rylan's drawer. I wasn't even sure if he had noticed it was missing.

I tugged the shirt over my head, the hem hitting me mid-thigh, and eyed my bed. But my stomach had other things in mind. The growling noise sounded like a mix between a werewolf howl and a screaming toddler.

"Damn," I murmured. A trip to the grocery store was on my list of things to do today, but the weather had been too lovely to pass up when I arrived home.

Trudging to the kitchen, I opened the small pantry and smirked. It wasn't full, but there was still my favorite cereal, some canned vegetables, and some packets of Ramen. And like any other college kid, the Ramen won.

I wasn't patient enough to wait for the water to boil on the stove. Instead, I followed the directions for cooking in the microwave and waited eagerly for the noodles to finish. The microwave beeped and I used my oven mitts to grab the bowl, careful of my wounded palms. Previous experience grabbing the bowl with bare hands proved that it would be hot as hell.

"Mmmm," I groaned as I carried the bowl to my coffee table. Snagging the remote, I queued up a movie to watch and stirred the noodles as I sat down.

It didn't take me long to devour the Ramen and I quickly made a second pack. I'd eaten two donuts with Gina this morning, which was more than I usually indulged in, but I suspected being in the sun and Eddie's unexpected visit triggered my appetite.

The second bowl tasted just as good as the last and I had to forcibly stop myself from making a third bowl. With the salt intake, I knew I'd regret it in the morning when I was bloated and my jeans wouldn't buckle.

After washing the bowl, I didn't even bother going back to my bedroom. I casually draped the blanket on the back of the sofa over my body and rested on the couch. Ryan Reynolds was on the screen in a blue shirt while his love interest explained that he was in a video game. Before I knew it, I'd fallen asleep before I saw the ending.

CHAPTER TEN
RYLAN

"**I**'m crashing your dinner."

We were boarding the plane, ready to fly back to Boston. Luckily it wasn't going to be as cold as it was when we left, but I'd miss the heat of Florida.

"No, you're not. You have dinner with your mom," Jolee pointed out. And she was absolutely right, but I wanted, needed to see Haley. It took everything in me to not message her every day, all day, while I was away. I wondered if the kiss before I left affected her the way it had affected me.

"I'm sure Mom won't mind," I replied as I took my seat beside Tyler. Mom was sitting in front of us and she turned around, a snarl on her perfectly made-up lips.

"I would too mind. It's upsetting enough that my girls don't want to join us. We're all still on vacation until tomorrow at 8 am."

Jolee, Sarah, and Keeley, who sat in the seats across the aisle from me, had the decency to look defeated. They quickly agreed to be at dinner tonight and reschedule with Haley. Mom insisted Haley join us, but we all knew she would decline.

But by them coming to dinner, I had no way to sneak out and see her without the entire group knowing. My brothers never paid enough attention to what was going on around them to notice if I was missing. And Mom was usually in the kitchen keeping track of five unruly adult men.

The plane ride was pretty quick, about three hours, and when we landed, the group of us gathered into the oversized van Mom had called.

"Hey, Mom?"

"Yes, Rylan?"

"I need to run by my apartment, but I'll be back for dinner."

"Okay. But please see if you can convince Haley to join us. And you better be on time."

"Yes, ma'am."

Closing my eyes, I leaned my head against the back of the seat, trying my damnedest to ignore the conversation behind me, but the girls had no sense of an inside voice. From what I could ascertain, Haley wasn't responding to their texts or calls. I wanted to tell them that sometimes people were busy, but I didn't want them to know that I was eavesdropping.

A slap sounded as a tanned hand landed on my shoulder. I pried my eyes open and turned to find Keeley leaning over the back of my seat.

"Do you think you can check on Haley? See if she responds to a message from you?"

"Guys, it's only nine in the morning. We left at five-thirty. She's probably still sleeping."

I knew from experience that Haley was not a morning person and would sleep until noon if the opportunity presented itself. But the group didn't need to know that intimate detail.

"But her phone is always on. Please."

"Fine."

Grumbling, I reached into my back pocket and lifted my phone, using my thumb to open the messaging app.

Me: Your friends are weird. Answer their messages.

"We're not weird. Just concerned, Rylan."

"Whatever. I'm trying to get a few more minutes of sleep, probably like your friend, if you don't mind."

From behind me, another voice said, "You don't have to be so grumpy about it."

By the time we arrived at Mom's house, Haley still hadn't returned my message or the girls'. I tried not to seem alarmed, but I'd be lying if I wasn't worried. They were right. It was rare that she didn't return a message.

I didn't even need to acknowledge the girls' pleading stares as I hopped into Link's car, which he offered to let me borrow. I had zero need to buy a car for myself. With a promise to let them know that Haley was safe and sound at her apartment, I headed out.

My fingers tapped nervously on the steering wheel during the drive to the complex, and when I arrived, my energy was zapping with anxiety. I was a live wire shooting sparks. Slamming the car into park, I barely remembered to grab the keys as I exited the vehicle. I'd come back to get my luggage.

Another student held the doors open to the complex for me and I mumbled my thanks as I made my way up the stairs, two at a time. When I got to the second floor, my heart stopped beating. She was standing in a black and red dress, holding a brown paper bag as she worked her key into the lock on the door.

"Haley," I whimpered. I liked to think the sound was due to my shortness of breath, but I knew it was due to the relief of finding her standing there unharmed.

"Rylan? What are you doing here?"

Standing at the top of the stairs, I needed a moment to take her in. The sun was gleaming brightly from the window at the end of the hall. She looked like a fucking angel come to life as it shone behind her head.

"Holy hell, you're beautiful."

"Um. . .thanks? Are you okay?"

"Yeah," I said as I finally got a handle on myself and walked toward her. She stepped inside her apartment and held the door open for me. As she slipped by me and went into her kitchen, she sat the bag of groceries on the counter with a thud.

"Is that everything?" I asked her, unsure if her ride-share was still waiting in the lot.

"No, I have two more in my car."

"You have a car?"

"Yeah, I brought it back with me."

"Where are the keys? I can get them for you."

She reached into the crevice between her breasts and revealed a single key fob with the Audi symbol. Damn, that was sexy as hell.

"What else you got in there?"

Chuckling, which only drew my attention even more to her chest, she shoved me toward the door. "You'll never know. It's the white one, by the way."

Quickly I located her car in the back corner of the lot under a light post and retrieved the two additional bags of groceries from the trunk. The lock engaged with a whoosh and I made it back to her apartment.

The door was still ajar and I closed it behind myself after entering. Wordlessly I began unloading her groceries and placed them where I remembered finding them before. It felt almost domestic.

Five packs of Ramen noodles sat at the bottom of one bag and I found myself laughing as I placed them on the shelf in her pantry.

Haley quickly explained that she had been craving them since she came home.

I felt my phone buzz in my pocket and the screen showed a message from Jolee asking about

Haley. It seemed I had failed at my mission already. I quickly texted back that she was good as gold.

"The girls were worried you didn't answer your phone."

"Oh! That reminds me, I need to go get a new one. I fell yesterday and the edge of my phone shattered. I didn't think anything of it, but it never charged overnight, so something must have been knocked loose."

"You fell? Are you okay?" I asked, ignoring the bushel of bananas in my grasp and moving closer to her. Haley gathered a bunch of material from her long dress and exposed her knees. There were darkened scabs along her shins and the signs of some bruising.

Kneeling on the floor, I placed the bananas by my feet as I reached out to examine her injuries more closely.

"I scraped up my hands too, but I'm ok. I actually tripped up the steps, if you can believe it."

"You're not usually so clumsy," I said, unable to move my fingers from behind her knees. The skin was so soft.

"I know, but I was looking down at my phone and missed the third step. And. . .um. . ." I gazed up at her and noticed she was biting her bottom lip.

"What is it?"

"It was nothing. Eddie was here, seeing someone on another floor. He wanted to apologize for how he acted."

Reflexively I gripped the back of her legs, wishing they were Eddie's neck. "He didn't do this, did he?"

"No, Rylan," she clarified, placing a gentle hand on my shoulder. "I really did just miss the step. Okay?"

It took me a moment to release the anger, but Haley's gentle hand on my shoulder acted as my talisman drawing me away from the rage.

Releasing her legs, I grabbed the bananas and finished emptying the bags of groceries.

By the time I finished emptying her groceries, I had turned to find Haley leaning against the counter, her face a bit paler than usual, which was saying something, because the girl could give a ghost a run for its money.

"Are you feeling okay, Hales?"

Shaking her head slightly, the ends of her hair brushing against her chest, she assured me that she was okay. "I have a lot on my mind."

"Want to talk about it? You should know," I began as I inched toward her, grabbing her hand because there was no way I could keep from touching her after being apart for a week. "If you say no, I will have to drag you to Mom's for dinner. If you agree, well, you're still going because, honestly, your friends scare me. Especially Sarah. She makes you think she's quiet and innocent, but I know that red hair means she has a temper like a firecracker."

A burst of laughter exploded from Haley as she interlaced her fingers with mine and guided me toward her couch.

We sat next to one another, but a good foot or two separated us. No part of us touched and it felt like an ocean between us. I hated this distance and I couldn't figure a way to navigate us closer.

"You don't have to tell me anything, cat."

"No, I do. I need to tell someone or I'm likely to go mad."

In an attempt to lighten the mood, I told her she was mad enough for the both of us already. When she giggled I held my hand out to her and she grasped it like a lifeline.

After a deep breath, she told me about her father's trial, the allegations from Senator Hastings' daughter, and how Hastings had propositioned her mother, which prompted the entire debacle.

The tale was so crazy that I didn't believe it at first. She must have noticed the skeptical expression on my face; her story read like a thriller, not a real-world occurrence. She pointed to a folder sitting on the edge of the coffee table. She urged me to sift through it, and there it all was. Every detail, every article, every deposition for anyone to see. Hastings had tried to bury it all, but private investigators knew how to work around red tape.

A picture of Haley's mother fell on my lap and I immediately recognized the resemblance between the two. Haley had her father's dark hair, but her facial features were exactly like her mother's.

"You look just like her, you know."

Quietly, Haley replied, "You think?"

"She was beautiful. Just like you."

"Flatterer." She paused for a moment and then tucked the picture back inside the folder with the rest of the contents. "I'm. . .I'm not sure that I'm up to seeing Ford and Keeley. I know that they had nothing to do with it, but I'm not sure that I can separate them from their birth father right now."

Her words hit home for me. Wasn't that similar to why I hadn't wanted to travel to Florida? Memories of that despicable human being almost kept me from enjoying one of the best vacations I had ever had with my family. I didn't want Haley to pull away from the people who loved her because of someone else's depravity.

"You know how I almost didn't go to Florida and gave you some lame excuse? Hell, I don't even remember what I said."

"I remember. I'm glad you went, though."

"The reason I wasn't going to go. . ." God, this was so hard. I couldn't bring myself to tell Jolee, but I cared about Haley and that changed everything. Taking a deep, shuddering breath, I continued. "I wasn't going to go because the man that raped me when I was ten lives there."

"Oh, Rylan!" Haley cried out as she launched herself at me. She wrapped her arms around my shoulders, sinking her head against my neck, and it felt like hugging an angel sent to take away all of your burdens.

"He was the father at my first foster home and abused his power. There were four of us kids in that home. He abused us all. It only happened to me once. I called my social worker in the middle of the night and she immediately got me out of there. I was lucky enough to have a good one on my side."

"What happened to the other kids?" Haley whispered against my neck.

"I don't know. I wish I did, but they were all shuffled around after the trial and the asshole moved to Florida. If it weren't for Mom, I don't know what I would do."

Tilting her head to rest on my shoulder, Haley stared out her glass doors. There was more to the story, but I wasn't ready to share that part of me yet. I wasn't sure I would ever be ready.

"I'm sorry that happened to you, Rylan. I wish I could save the little boy that you were."

Kissing the top of her head, I flexed my fingers around her hand. "Thank you."

"You're right, though. I can't hide from my friends because their father was an asshole."

"Ford would tell you that the man was a sperm donor only."

Haley mumbled under her breath and then lifted her feet onto the couch, angling her body against mine.

"I'm exhausted. I've been sleeping like crazy since I got back."

Gently I slipped from underneath her and settled the rest of her body on the couch. I kissed her cheek, her purple eyes already shut and her breathing evening out.

"I'll be back in an hour and we'll go grab you a new phone before going to dinner, okay?"

"Mhmm," she mumbled in her sleep.

Before leaving, I snagged the extra copy of her apartment key dangling on a hook in the kitchen and went back to Link's car to grab my luggage. I knew how tiring it was to have your life flipped upside down. I remember sleeping for three days straight when I learned my parents left me. And with school, Haley needed her rest.

My apartment looked just the way I left it and after tossing my clothes in the washer, I grabbed a bottle of water from the fridge. The water wasn't what I wanted, a bottle of Jack would have done the trick, but I needed to drive later. And Haley's life was too important to me.

Shit, I felt myself slipping into new territory with her. Neither of us was in the right headspace for anything more than sex, that was why we both took that step back, but I craved her kisses and touch.

Needing a distraction, I shed my clothes and hopped into the shower, the pressure of the spray tingling my skin like tiny pinpricks. If only the heat of the water could melt the frozen heart inside my chest. It's what kept my armor in place, forced me to keep a distance from everyone.

Luckily Haley was waking up when I let myself into her apartment. The dark smudges under her eyes were concerning, but she assured me that she was okay. With graduation in a month and a half we all had a lot on our minds.

I had my summer internship lined up, but I wasn't sure what Haley's plans were. When I asked in her car, she shrugged and guided us to the parking lot for the phone store.

It didn't take her long to find a new phone and have her information transferred over. Despite arguing with me, she allowed me to drive her car to Mom's house.

When we arrived, the house was empty. Because of the warm weather, everyone had ventured to the back patio. My brothers were in a rigorous game of football while the girls chatted in lounge chairs beside the pool. It was still under the cover, but Mom would be opening it up soon enough.

"Hey, everyone," I called out, bringing their attention over to Haley and me. She took a step back as the girls approached excitedly. It would have been comical had she not dug her nails into my arm.

"Save me," Haley whispered as Jolee reached her first.

"You'll be fine."

"Traitor." She snarled as Jolee pulled her toward the chairs they had vacated.

It didn't take long for my brothers to rope me into the game, and before long, Mom called us inside for dinner.

Haley sat beside me, and I felt a sense of peace at the table for the first time. Unable to control myself, I leaned over to whisper in her ear. "I want to slip under the table and eat your pussy until you can't see straight." She was my favorite dessert, after all.

Across from me, Chance cocked one of his eyebrows and pointed his fork loaded with a slice of meatloaf in my direction. "Ry, is there something you want to share with the rest of the table?"

"No. I'm good." I ignored his taunt.

"Are you sure? Because whatever you said to Haley has her blushing like a sinner in church. And I think we'd all like to hear what caused that coloring."

Mom spoke up and admonished my brother for embarrassing Haley and then agreed that I shouldn't tell secrets at the table.

An interruptive cough brought my attention to Haley, and with a devilish grin, she said, "Rylan was just mentioning how excited he was to hear me practice my piece for the showcase. Next Saturday, there is a school charity event, and I was asked to play."

"Oh, Rylan," my mother spoke up before I could bolt from the table. "It's so wonderful for you to escort Haley."

The rest of the group looked skeptical, but the topic was forgotten as Mom changed the conversation to Jolee's wildlife sanctuary.

Leaning toward Haley again, I growled in her ear, "I'm going to spank your ass later for that."

A piece of apple pie sits delicately on the edge of her fork as she looks at me. "I'm looking forward to it."

CHAPTER ELEVEN
HALEY

Shit.

I was late.

Not like late to class or late to pick up a package. Late as in, I'd missed my last two periods. Menstrual cycles. Visits from Aunt Flow. I was never good at calculating my cycles, but they averaged between twenty-eight and thirty-seven days. I didn't even realize I'd never had one while I was home on spring break because, hello, personal drama.

Then when I turned on my phone this morning, I had an alert from my tracking app that I needed to log my last cycles. Two cycles.

I had no idea what to do. The stress from the last couple of weeks could've been the culprit, but I'd also had *a lot* of sex with Rylan.

Should I reach out to my friends and ask them for advice? Go to the student health center? Maybe a trip to the emergency room?

My inner thoughts were driving me nuts.

Leaving class, I decided to skip the next, a psychology course for my minor that I was already acing, and head to a drug store over in the next town. I didn't know why I cared so much if anyone saw me, but I didn't want word to get back to Rylan or my friends until I had a concrete answer.

It took an hour to get to Braintree, clear on the other side of Boston. My GPS guided me to a local drug store and I picked up three different types of tests. One was digital, one was with the lines I always saw on television and in movies, and the last was a cup with a stick. I knew somehow I'd fuck that one up.

Before going to the register, I walked down the snacks aisle and grabbed a few of my favorites. Sour gummy worms, Sweet Tarts, and Skittles; I was a sugary sweets person and if I was going to have the news that I suspected, I planned on indulging. At the last minute, I snagged a large Gatorade and headed toward the register. The woman working smiled at me as she rang up the items, not once giving me a pitiful look that I had suspected.

I swiped my card at the total and grasped the bag's handles.

"Good luck, sweetie. Whatever it says, everything will be fine."

I blamed the hormones, but tears immediately leaked from the corners of my eyes. "Thank you."

I stopped for some fast food on my way back to campus and was glad that I put something in my stomach because when I arrived home, I was sure that I was going to throw up. And I hated dry heaves more than I hated actually vomiting.

I chugged the Gatorade I purchased and sat on my couch with the bag on my lap. My soft chuckle hummed in the quiet room and it sounded like the whistle of a thousand locomotives.

I was trying my damnedest not to jump to conclusions, but I was fairly positive about what those tests were going to say. My entire college career was going to be one more statistic.

After about thirty minutes of staring at the blank television screen, I decided to test my luck and headed to the bathroom. The directions on the tests were simple enough, even the one I was certain to mess up.

After setting everything on the counter, I went into my bedroom and set the timer on my phone. A message from Rylan came across my phone asking what he needed to wear to the charity event the next day. It was black-tie, and when I had invited him, well, forced his hand to take me, I hadn't even considered the attire.

> **Me: It's black-tie. Do you have something? It may be too late to rent. I'm sorry, I wasn't thinking.**

> **Rylan: No worries, cat. I have something. I'm not destitute you know.**

Rylan was one of the lucky kids that made it into a family of wealth. Not that Dr. Fincher was a millionaire, but her late husband had a hefty life insurance policy, and Tracy also was from a long-established banker family. Well, maybe she was a millionaire. The guys weren't spoiled, though. They took jobs in the summer and worked hard for their degrees. It made me happy to know that they'd always have a support system in their mom.

In that aspect, Rylan and I weren't so different. Dad made good money with his career and Mom's family had been oil tycoons in Texas for generations. She had established a trust fund for me as a child that I gained access to when I turned twenty. And though I'd take her being alive over any life insurance policy, she and dad ensured that if something happened to either of them, I'd be set for life.

Girls in my high school never understood my desire to go to college and get a job. They assumed that I'd become a socialite in the big cities since I had money to burn. But I enjoyed working and being busy.

Jarring me from my thoughts, the buzzer on my phone went off. Blankly I stared at the offended mobile device in my hand and wondered if I could ignore everything and continue my day as if I wasn't about to learn whether I would be a parent.

Crap.

Rylan texted again, this time a meme of Mugatu's models in *Zoolander*. It was his Derelicte line.

Me: I dare you.

Rylan: You're on.

I tossed my phone onto the bed; the soft duvet didn't even move when it landed, just absorbed the weight. I knew that I had wasted enough time. I wondered if the tests were only good for a specific time period. You had exactly five minutes to look or they were all changing to positive.

"Suck it up, buttercup," I whispered to myself and made my way to the bathroom. I covered my eyes with my hand as I blindly flicked on the light and tilted my head down.

"On three. One. Two." I was never patient enough to make it to three. Forcing my hand away, I stared down at the three tests on my bathroom vanity, confirming what I already knew.

I was going to be a mom.

After a few deep breaths, I decided to reach out to the girls and asked them if they could come over for some pizza tonight, then brought up the number on my phone for my OBGYN. I had no idea how far along I was, but I did know the last date of my period, which was a couple of weeks after I returned from Europe. At least I could say that I hadn't been knocked up during my first time having sex.

The nurse made me an appointment for Monday afternoon when she estimated that I was most likely ten weeks along, which meant that I needed to decide if I wanted to tell Rylan before or after the appointment. I had no reference in gauging how he would react to the news. Rylan was one of those people that ran hot then cold. Some days he acted like I was his entire world and he couldn't get enough of being with me. Those days I'd hoped that he would open up more. But then he'd run ice cold the next, barely making contact.

It was exhausting.

If anyone knew what I should do, it would be my friends, and I was confident that they'd keep my secret until I was ready.

Despite the shape my head was in, I grabbed my bag and trudged across campus to finish my classes for the day. I needed to attend philosophy so that Rylan wouldn't suspect anything. Even as he sat on the other side of the classroom, I felt his stare the entire time. I'd wondered if he could tell that something had changed and that our lives would completely transform.

"Haley!" he called out before I'd left my seat, attracting the gazes of some of our classmates.

I tried to mask my nervousness by gripping the strap of my bag as I waited for him to approach. The leather cut into my palms, but I welcomed the pain.

"Hey, cat," he said as we turned to walk out of the room together.

"Did you need help finding your suit?" I joked. "There is a dumpster behind the apartment we could rummage through."

Rylan laughed, one of those carefree chuckles that had every woman within a five-mile radius taking notice. I loved when he let down his guard. Looking up at him as he tossed his arm over my shoulders, a wide grin on his face, I knew that I had fallen in love with him. This model perfect man had demons to battle. The man that had sworn off love. He wore his darkness like armor. Heavy. Impenetrable. And I feared if he ever did allow himself to love, he would wield it like a dagger.

Soon the grin fell from his face and he looked down at me with concern. "Why are you looking at me like that?" he asked.

"No reason. I was just thinking about something for the performance tomorrow. I need to prepare two hours' worth of music."

"Wow, that's a lot. You aren't going to be disappointed if I need to distract myself every once in a while, are you? Music is just. . .hard for me sometimes."

I'd asked him before why he'd never listened to the radio or asked me to play the song he inspired. He'd mentioned that music reminded him of something he lost and left it at that.

"I know. I understand and I'm thankful you still wanted to come with me. You don't have to."

"Sure I do," he huffed. "I don't want you asking pretty boy from class or one of my brothers."

"Jealous?" I asked, poking him just below the ribs. "If you weren't going with me, I'd just go by myself. No need to worry."

The buildings holding the business department came into view as we turned a corner in the path and I felt Rylan tense up. The group from the study abroad program was gathered at the edge of the stairs looking like they had just come back from a meeting with the CEO of a Fortune 500 company and were ready to tell anyone who would listen. I never understood how someone like Rylan could be friendly with those guys. They came off like the sleezy guys that went to prep school, but Rylan was much more laid-back. But maybe they had things in common that I didn't understand.

As we got closer, Rylan dropped his arm from around my shoulder and took a step back while the CEO squad looked onward.

"Uh, okay," I scoffed. Did he think that I wouldn't notice the change in him?

Rylan ran a hand down his face before he turned to face me. "Hey, it's not like that, okay. They're just. . ."

"I think it's just like that. You're ashamed to be seen with me, but whatever, it's not like we're together anyway."

I turned to walk away, but Rylan grabbed my elbow and twisted me back toward him. "Look, I'm not ashamed of you at all. It's just those guys are freaking assholes. I'm going to be late for class. Can we talk about this tonight?"

Remembering the reason I made a trip across the city today; I shook my head. "I'm having a pizza night with the girls."

"Well, tomorrow at least, but I'd really like to see you tonight."

"Maybe. It's not like you don't know where I live."

Smirking, Rylan released his hold on my elbow and walked backward down the pathway. "Bye, cat!" he called out, alerting some of the passing females of his presence.

I would have been embarrassed had not more than one of those girls not called out, "You can pet my kitty anytime," causing Rylan to almost trip up the stairs.

I anxiously paced my living room waiting for my friends to arrive as the recently delivered pizza sat on my coffee table. I wasn't sure if they would be able to look at me and tell that something was different or if they would snoop through my trash for whatever reason, but I was a nervous wreck.

My palms were sweaty, so I shook my hands and then wiped them on my black jeans. God, I was going to have to buy new clothes. I hate clothes shopping. I needed to check online and see when I'd outgrow my current clothes. Would I ever go back to my normal size? And what about my breasts? They were already more sensitive than before. Were they ever going to be normal again?

A knock sounded and I sent a silent thank you to the heavens before dashing to the door. Jolee came strutting into the room with a bottle of her favorite red wine hoisted in the air. Keeley and Sarah followed behind with their own bottles of white wine.

The girls made their way to my kitchen and reached for the wine glasses in the upper cabinet by the fridge as they'd done so many times. Keeley grabbed a second glass and asked if I planned on having white or red.

My eyes darted at my friends in various states of opening and pouring wine.

Unable to hold back, I blurted, "I'm pregnant."

The glass in Keeley's hand fell to the floor and shattered around her feet.

"Oh my gosh, don't move," I told her as I went to my laundry room and grabbed the broom and dust pan. Silently the girls stood as I cleaned up the mess.

They seemed to be in a higher state of shock than I had been when I took the tests.

"Okay, I think that's all of it."

Jolee was the first to crack. "Uh. I'm sorry, let's start this over. You're pregnant? As in missed a period. . ."

"As in missed two periods, took three tests, which were positive, and I have an appointment on Monday."

Sarah calmly walked over and grasped my hand. I wasn't sure how she knew that I needed a bit of comfort at that moment. "How far along are you?"

"Maybe ten weeks? I won't know until Monday."

She guided me to my couch, where the smell of pizza wafted from the boxes on my coffee table. "How are you feeling?" Sarah asked as she sat beside me. Jolee hurried to the open seat on my opposite side and Keeley folded her legs criss-cross style and sat on the floor.

"Um, good, considering I had no idea. I've just been tired, but I figured that was stress with midterms and graduation looming."

"What do you think you'll do?" Keeley questioned, her eyes pinned to me. "Are you going to keep it?"

Strangely it was the first time I'd even considered whether I would keep the baby or not. In my mind, there was only the option to continue with the pregnancy. Gently I placed my hand on my stomach and smiled. "Yeah, I'm going to keep it." I wasn't a young girl that was still a baby herself. My mom wasn't much older when she and my father had me.

"Well, I can't wait to be Auntie Jolee. What did Rylan say when you told him?"

"I haven't told him yet. Honestly, it didn't feel real until just now. You guys are the first to know."

A pause met each of our ears before Keeley quietly inquired, "You are going to tell him, though, right? Like soon?"

"Yeah, I just. . . He's so closed off and changes the subject whenever I ask him about his family. I'll tell him, but I'm scared of what his reaction may be.

"But, I think I'll tell him tomorrow. He's going with me to that charity event and I'll let him decide if he wants to come with me to the appointment Monday."

"That's a good idea. We're behind you one hundred percent, whatever you decide," Jolee chimed in. The girls echoed her remarks.

"Why don't you guys go pour yourself the wine you brought. Obviously, I'm not partaking. I'll bring out the dress my dad's girlfriend picked out for me. I may hate clothes, but I love this dress."

As expected, the girls go a little nutty for the designer gown. It's a black strapless design with a full skirt and a rhinestone belt, but the best part was the hidden pockets. I think all dresses should come with pockets.

"You're going to drive him crazy when he sees you in that tomorrow."

"Or I'll drive him away when I tell him that I'm having his baby."

Jolee eyes me as I fold the top of the dress over my arms. "I think Rylan has a complicated past and he makes himself just out of reach for a reason. I'm not saying he will react badly, but there is a good chance whatever happened with his birth parents is going to affect any decisions he makes. You just need to give him time, okay.

"I can absolutely assure you that you will not be left to fend for yourself with the baby. We will all be here and so will his brothers. It may be unconventional, but we're one heck of a family."

It had to be the hormones. That was the only explanation for me falling to my knees in a heap with the dress cradled in my arms. I wept like a lunatic. My wonderful friends knelt beside me and rubbed my back while offering comforting words. I'd been an only child, wishing every night for a sibling or two but never been graced with any, then these perfect women came into my life and gave me the support and love that only a family could provide.

I was so fucking lucky.

And so scared I would lose them all, especially Rylan, the one that couldn't love me back.

CHAPTER TWELVE
RYLAN

Staring in the mirror, I had to remind myself that I was doing this for Haley, and it was good practice for all of the weddings my brothers would be having in the next few years.

But damn, I hated wearing the penguin suit.

Link was chilling in my living room, and I called out his name because if I had to mess with the damn bow tie one more time, I would rip it off and burn it.

"Well, brother, you clean up pretty good. I can't say I've ever seen you in a tuxedo before."

Wordlessly I pointed to the damn piece of black material hanging around my neck, hoping that he would get the hint.

"Never went to prom. So, this would be the first."

"Aw, should I take some pictures of you and your date in front of the stairs?"

"You're an asshole."

"I know," he replied, fiddling with the tie until it sat just right.

"Thanks."

I brushed by him and went into my bathroom to try and tame my hair. It had grown a bit longer than I usually kept it, but I couldn't lie and say I didn't enjoy it when Haley would snake her fingers in the strands and tug.

God, when was the last time I'd had sex with her? Before spring break? Too long. My cock stood at attention whenever we were in a room together, which would make me look like a fool with these suit pants and a tent forming all night.

Flipping the lid to a bottle of gel, I poured some of the contents into the palm of my hands and wove it through the strands, just enough to keep it off my face. I looked like a more polished and presentable version of myself.

"Alright, do I pass?" I asked Link as I stepped from the bathroom back into my bedroom.

"You look good. Remember to have fun tonight. And maybe get back in Haley's good graces."

"We are friends again. Hello. I'm going with her tonight."

"You know what I mean. You two can make things work in an actual relationship."

"Ugh. . .and where is your girlfriend, oh mighty one?" I jested as I grabbed my wallet.

I didn't need to borrow Link's keys since we rented a town car for the event. We didn't want to show up at the five-star luxury hotel in just any car.

Link ushered me out the door and went to his apartment next door, ignoring my jab.

Quickly I went down to Haley's apartment and knocked on the door. I hadn't been sure what to expect. Haley was, after all, a girl that lived in black and rarely wore a face full of makeup. I loved her style and attitude, but I equally loved this woman who opened the door.

Haley looked like a fucking knockout and I stared at her, completely stunned. The dress was simple yet showed off all of her curves that I loved. It was even better than that damn red dress she wore to dinner with her father. I'd jerked off to images of her in that dress for weeks.

"You are. . .breathtaking, Haley. Fucking hell, I'm not going to be able to keep my hands off of you."

Haley giggled as she reached for a small bag that sparkled in her hand as it hit the light. "That's okay. I won't mind if you don't."

"You can't tell me things like that or we'll never leave your apartment."

"Sorry, but the car is already here and I need to be ready to play at eight. I get an hour to warm up beforehand."

I incoherently mumbled as she shut her door and offered her my arm to escort her down the stairs. Link had joked about going to prom, but that was exactly how this felt. Should I have bought her a corsage too?

Mustering up any manners I'd ever been taught, mostly by Tracy, I held the door for Haley when we entered and exited the car. When we arrived at the hotel, I was surprised to see so many Wellington students and faculty attending, especially before the event was slated to begin.

"Wow, there are a lot of people here," Haley mumbled beside me as my fingers reached out for hers. She quickly latched on and I savored her touch.

"You're going to be spectacular."

Together we scoped out the event's surroundings, quickly locating the piano and guitar tucked away in the corner. I knew she played piano, but I'd never considered if she was fluent in other instruments. The setup had her almost completely blocked off from view. That was a shame because she was going to be stunning behind the instruments.

"Do you play the guitar too?" I asked as we passed a table of hors d'oeuvres, snagging a few of the miniature quiches. I never understood the tiny foods meant to hold people over for hours. A man needs to eat.

"I do. Not as well as the piano, but I've practiced that one much longer. Want to know a secret?"

"You're not wearing panties?"

Haley playfully shoved me and I acted as if she'd hit me with the force of Muhammed Ali. She blushed as my overzealous reaction caused a few people to sneer in our direction.

"You'll never know if I am or not now, buddy."

"Shame."

"As I was saying. I know how to read sheet music and such, but I can play almost anything by ear. My piano teacher said I was one of the lucky few. To be honest, it's a little irritating."

"How so?" I was completely intrigued.

"Well, usually when I've heard the song before, especially something on the radio, and then I have the sheet music in front of me, they aren't always the same. And it can be infuriating when you argue with someone about which way is correct."

"Wow, I can imagine how difficult that could be."

I was honest because I couldn't imagine having the ability to do either, but Haley took it as another jab at her and shoved me playfully. Unfortunately, her shove landed me against one of the arrogant women walking around showcasing all of the costume jewelry she wanted everyone to believe was real.

I mumbled my apologies and the woman huffed as she walked away.

"Troublemaker," I hissed at Haley, who had the decency to laugh behind her hand.

Continuing to walk around the room, Haley left her hand resting in the crease of my elbow as we greeted the few people we knew. Soon she led me to a side room where there was a piano and guitar set, ready for her to practice.

"Thank you, Rylan, for coming with me tonight. You look great in that tux, by the way."

"Well, I'll have to find more reasons to wear it then." She smiled up at me, the warmth of her gesture melting the metal of my armor. She was picking it apart piece by piece, and I knew she had no idea. "Are you nervous?" I questioned as we slid behind the piano toward the bench. No one was paying us any mind.

"Maybe a little. It's not the first time I've played for a crowd like this, but it's been a while." Haley scooted onto the bench, perching on the very edge closest to the piano, and splayed her gown out on either side of her until it draped over the entire bench.

I took that as my cue to fall back, but instead of joining the crowd that seemed to grow, I leaned against one of the pillars within an arm's reach of her. Her eyes closed as she placed her fingers gently on the keys, then she started playing. Haley was intoxicating to watch. I didn't even hear the music; I was drawn to how her entire body played out the song. She didn't just rely on her fingers, her body swayed to the music and her feet pumped the pedals.

I hated music for the things it reminded me that I lost, but I could watch Haley play for hours.

She only paused for a beat before diving into another song and then another. I was overcome with jealousy at sharing her talent with these people that couldn't care less about the gift she was giving them.

We'd only been here twenty minutes and I was growing antsy, ready to call it a night. This time it had nothing to do with music and everything to do with Haley. She had hypnotized me with her melody. I was entranced. I saw no one but her and needed no one but her.

Glancing over her shoulder, Haley winked in my direction before she pulled her fingers away from the keys and sat back on the bench. She stood and skirted around the bench before coming to face me, a smile growing, her purple eyes shining against her pale skin.

I'd snagged a glass of water for her from a passing server a few minutes prior and she graciously accepted before swallowing it in a few unladylike gulps. I practically waited with bated breath to hear her burp, but luckily she handed me the glass back and gave me a quick kiss on my cheek as thanks.

"You're remarkable, Haley. I've enjoyed watching you play."

"Really? You're not ready to duck out and leave me stranded?"

"No way. Honestly, I could watch you play all day. I may tune out the music, but you're enthralling to watch." Leaning closer, I whispered in her ear, exposed by her hair twisted and hanging over one delectable breast. "You had my dick standing at attention the minute your fingers stroked those keys."

"Rylan," she moaned as my lips caressed the outer edge of her ear.

"Tell me, cat. Can you play that thing without the pedals?"

"Of course." She pulled back and looked at me quizzically. "Why?"

"When you sit down, make sure you're as close to the edge as possible and don't play with the pedals. If you're a good girl, maybe I'll return the favor for turning me on with your skills."

She nodded, her eyes glazed over as she went back to the piano bench and situated herself and her dress accordingly. She glanced back over her shoulder at me with her fingers on the ivories. I winked and leaned against the pillar again.

From my view out to the lobby, I noticed the crowd had begun moving toward some of the auctioned pieces to view their selections. The auction would take place in another room soon. It was enough time to spur into action.

I walked closer to Haley and then crouched down, crawling on my hands and knees between the piano and bench seat. I didn't even care that I was probably ruining my pants. That's why they had dry cleaners.

As I lifted her fluffy skirt, I noticed the strappy heels on her feet and swore under my breath, which elicited a giggle from Haley. I wanted to fuck her wearing nothing else but those shoes. With the skill of a ninja, I slipped completely under her skirt and waited for the material to pool around me. My shoes were probably sticking out, but I didn't care when the most beautiful pussy was before me.

She wasn't bare underneath her dress as she had joked earlier, but I could see that she was wearing something lacy even in the darkness.

I slid my hands up her thighs, which she gloriously parted even wider for me until my thumbs reached her wet center. For a moment, I wondered if I should pull back as I gently rubbed at the material, which grew hotter under my thumb, but her answering moan told me everything that I needed to know. Haley was definitely on board.

My thumbs played on the outside of her panties. When she switched to a new song, I slipped my fingers on the inside of the material and tugged it aside. Unable to hold back, I slid my hands under her thighs and lifted her higher so that I could bring her to my mouth and feast. God, I wanted my mouth on those sweet lips.

My fucking cat never missed a beat.

Her legs quaked against my palms as I swirled my tongue around her sensitive nub. I knew she was close when she clenched her legs around my head. The burst of heat from her sex left my cock standing at attention.

Gently I placed her legs back on the bench and adjusted her panties as best as I could under the darkness of her dress. I was so lost in the taste of Haley that I wasn't sure if she'd messed up her song, but my cat was a professional and I was positive she was able to hide her orgasm.

I waited until she began another song, this one slow and sleepy, to crawl out from under her dress. Like a coward, I checked to make sure no one was looking in the room, not for my sake but Haley's.

Once I freed myself, I stood and brushed off my pants and jacket and twisted my cufflink. If anyone noticed, they'd simply think I'd lost it. Making my way back to the pillar I'd come to claim as my own.

Effortlessly Haley continued to practice her set as if nothing amiss had occurred. How she did anything after an orgasm was beyond me. Sometimes I didn't even remember removing a condom afterward. My brain was usually fried.

"Rylan," Haley whispered from her stance, twisting her head just so.

I walked toward her and leaned over. "Yeah?"

"If you don't figure out a way to fuck me in the next fifteen minutes, I'm going to kill you." She reminded me of an animal in heat. Wild eyes, panting breaths. I fucking loved it.

"Aw, that one orgasm wasn't enough for you, cat?"

She didn't respond. Instead, she turned to face me, her fingers still working the keys, and sneered at me.

"Alright, let me see."

Glancing out at the lobby, I noticed more partygoers had arrived. But for the most part, we were completely alone.

Glancing down at my watch, I realized that Haley still had about twenty minutes left before her set. The guitar in the corner caught my eye. I cringed realizing that I was tempted to expose a part of myself, a piece I had long ago admonished, all for the chance to fuck Haley. But she was so tempting. Like the only drop of water in a desert.

I stood by Haley for another minute, her eyes closed, her body swaying gently to the music, and the softest of smirks on her lips.

Shit.

I stomped over to the guitar, strummed it twice, and then plugged it into the small amp. I didn't want to draw a lot of attention. The movement came naturally and I fucking despised it. I had to swallow the vomit that pooled in my mouth as the first notes hit my ear.

Haley's body jerked in surprise when she heard the guitar and when I whispered in her ear, "Stand up," she didn't question me.

I used my foot to quietly move the bench out of the way and stand behind Haley. "Finish the song," I demanded before I lost my blind courage.

She played the last notes on the piano and dropped her hands by her sides. I gently pushed her body until it rested on the top of the piano, her face tilted at a downward angle. Quickly, I reached out with my hand, bunched the side of her dress that wasn't exposed to the crowd, and lifted it to her waist, commanding her to hold it. She complied beautifully. I was about to do something that I had no clue would work, but my dick was guiding me at the moment. It would do anything to sink into Haley's hot pussy.

I unzipped my pants and freed my cock with swift work, then slipped her panties to the side, exposing her sex. I glided my shaft against her folds, whimpering as I remembered that I had no condom because why the hell would I need one at a charity event.

"I can't get pregnant right now," Haley assured me and my brain, still buzzing from her orgasm on my tongue earlier. I shifted my body until my erection slid deep inside her core.

As I moved in and out of her sheath, I cursed under my breath and then began to strum the guitar. An old Sex Pistols song my birth parents played on repeat and made sure I knew how to play on guitar by the age of six came to me like clockwork. We couldn't afford food, but we could afford the eight guitars that littered the dirty van we called home.

Here I was with the most gorgeous and gracious girl I'd ever met, letting me fuck her into tomorrow and I was playing guitar and thinking about my parents. I hadn't held a guitar since I was ten.

I began pounding into Haley, the tightness of her pussy gripping my shaft. Every once in a while, her body would press against a piano key. The angry tune playing on the guitar in my hand masked our heavy breaths.

Looking down at Haley, she started biting her lip; one of her tells that she was getting close, which was good because taking her bareback was the closest I'd ever been to heaven. Her walls were squeezing me and I felt myself coming as she shattered, her body growing lax against the piano.

Despite our exhaustion, I finished the song as I slipped my cock from her sex. She readjusted her panties and righted herself, releasing her dress at the same time while I zipped my pants and tucked my dress shirt back into place.

I was sure my brothers would never believe that I had just had sex against a piano in a hotel, but Haley would know. That was all that mattered.

As the song finished, I unplugged the instrument from the amp and set it back on the stand. Haley stood watching me in awe with her slightly mussed hair and rumpled dress. She seemed to care about her appearance as little as I did.

"So, you play guitar." She smirked.

"We're going to pretend you didn't see or hear that."

"I can't now! It will forever be etched in my brain. You do play beautifully, by the way."

"Well. . .try." We stared at each other and the realization hit me that this was the first time we'd had sex again since I asked for a break. "Um . . do you think they'd realize if you left early?"

"Yes. I still have to perform my set."

"Well, shit."

The two hours went by agonizingly slow, but finally, Haley turned on the stool when she hit the last note in a song.

Haley reached in her small bag for her phone and dialed the car service so they'd be waiting outside. After ensuring everything was back where we found it, I escorted Haley from the hotel and made the trip back to our complex.

She seemed dead on her feet as I helped her from the car. The performance must have taken a toll on her. I reached for her bag and dug out her keys when we approached her floor.

With a quick twist of my wrist, I unlocked her door and helped her inside. "Hales, can I help you with-" I began, wondering if she'd need help with her dress and about to ask if she wanted company in the shower.

"I'm pregnant."

CHAPTER THIRTEEN
HALEY

I hadn't planned on blurting it out while Rylan was eyeing me like his favorite steak served on a gold platter. I blamed my utter exhaustion. After playing the piano for two full sets and having two mind-blowing orgasms, I was spent in the best sense of the word.

"I'm sorry. I may not be the brightest bulb in the box, but I'm pretty sure that you wouldn't know you were pregnant from the sex we just had. I mean, sure, we should probab-" I held my finger up to Rylan's mouth to stop his chatter.

"Rylan, I'm really tired. We can discuss it more in the morning. Yes, I'm pregnant, about ten weeks or so. I took three tests yesterday to verify and I have an appointment on Monday. No, I didn't do it to trap you and I'm sorry it happened like this. I know you don't want to be tied down or have a relationship or-" Now it was his turn to cut me off.

Rylan pressed his lips against mine in a kiss like none I'd ever experienced. His tongue swirled around mine, tangoing to a song of our own. It was one of desire, joy, and possessiveness.

The fatigue I felt when we arrived home was whisked away by the brush of Rylan's mouth against my lips.

Callused hands grasped my face and Rylan pulled back to stare down at me. "I want to go with you to the appointment."

"Okay," I whispered. Another chaste kiss followed.

When I took the tests on Friday, I had been worried about his reaction; I think all females have the fear that the father would react negatively.

"Have you told anyone?"

"Just the girls." At his alarmed expression, I assured him that they would stick to the girl code and keep the secret. "I needed their advice. They're like sisters to me."

Rylan nodded and said he understood.

"Are you mad?" I asked him as I took a step back, turned on the small lamp on the table in the entryway, and placed my clutch on the top. I turned to face him and waited for his response focusing on his eyes. Despite whatever Rylan said, his eyes were a clear sign of what he was feeling. He had the most profound hazel eyes. They glowed a bright emerald green when he was angry and were almost brown when he was sad.

"I'm. . .I'm not sure how I feel, to be honest. But it's late, and as you said, we can talk in the morning. Are you. . .okay?" There was a look of concern on his face as his eyes twitched between looking at my face and my stomach almost broke my heart.

I reached out for his hand to reassure him. "I'm good, Rylan. Everything is good, I promise. It's late, and I know you're right upstairs, but do you want to stay the night?"

He was quiet for a while, to the point I was afraid he'd say no, but Rylan surprised me when he reached for my hand and guided me back toward my bedroom.

When we crossed the threshold, Rylan pressed his body against mine. "Turn around."

My hair was still draped over my shoulder, leaving the zipper down the back exposed. Rylan's fingers trailed a path down my back as he took an agonizingly slow time to drag the mechanism to the bottom. I hadn't worn a bra with the dress; just the black lace panties left exposed from the zipper.

His sudden hitch of breath shouldn't have been so satisfying, but I felt the corners of my lips tilting upward.

Rylan must have been practicing a tremendous amount of self-control because he moved around me, reached into the top drawer of my dresser, and tugged one of my sleeping shirts over my head. His eyes didn't even drop down to my breasts, which I knew he loved.

With a gentleness I had never experienced, Rylan bent his knees slightly and lifted me into his arms. He made the small trek to my bed and placed me in the spot I'd always claimed.

"Need anything?"

Silently I shook my head and tugged the covers bunched at the bottom of the bed over my exposed legs. Even through my exhaustion, my body felt like it was on fire as I watched Rylan remove his tuxedo jacket, unfastened each button of his dress shirt, slid it effortlessly off his upper body, and then dropped his pants to his ankles while toeing off his shoes and socks.

I'd never tire of admiring his muscular body. He was the perfect mix of bulky and lean and my tongue salivated as I focused on his eight-pack.

"Stop looking at me like that, babe," Rylan said as he made his way to the opposite side of the bed. My eyes tracked his movements the entire time.

"Can't help it. You're sexy."

His large body wiggled under the sheets and waited for me to press my backside against his. This was his favorite way to sleep with me, curled around my body like a cocoon.

"Rylan?"

"Hmm?" he mumbled against the top of my head.

"Are we going to be okay?"

"Yeah, cat. It will all work out."

The pending pregnancy loomed over our heads, but we spent the rest of the weekend avoiding the discussion. When we woke on Sunday morning, well, afternoon because it was closer to lunchtime, Rylan rolled me on top of him and we had sex for an hour straight. I couldn't get enough of his cock with my raging hormones, and I was pretty sure Rylan was fucking me to forget everything.

Rylan drove us in my car to my doctor's appointment. We made small talk, but I was so nervous

I'd almost asked him to pull over twice because I felt like I was going to be sick. When he parked outside the office, neither of us made a move to leave the confines of the car. Once I went in there and the doctor confirmed what I knew, it would all be real. I wondered if Rylan thought the same.

"I'm nervous," I told him. We arrived about twenty minutes ahead of time, and I was procrastinating as long as possible. The unanswered questions floated around my head. What if something was wrong with the baby? Or what if I wasn't pregnant and there was something wrong with me?

"Me too," he agreed as he placed his hand gently on my thigh. Instinctively I put my hand on top of his. Flipping his over, he wrapped his fingers through mine.

I watched as a couple began walking toward the entrance. They didn't appear much older than Rylan and me. The man had a protective arm around the girl, whom I realized was his wife by the shiny rock dangling from her ring finger as she cradled her large baby bump. I giggled as I realized that she was waddling. I'd always thought that was a myth. Pregnancy wasn't something to which I paid a lot of attention.

"You think you're ready to go in? We have about ten minutes."

Nodding, I released his hand and reached for the door handle, but Rylan asked me to wait. He dashed around the car and opened my door, holding out his hand to help me. We never really got around to any dating, so I wasn't sure if his manners were for show or if they'd been there all along and I'd just never been aware.

I was glad he was here with me today. As we walked into the reception area, I felt a dozen or so eyes land on me. If I'd been here alone, I would have turned right back around and left. But Rylan was my anchor.

"Don't worry about them, cat. They're just jealous that you're here with a sexy as fuck man and they're here with a shlump."

I giggled and the action completely put me at ease. "Your ego knows no bounds."

Rylan's hand landed on his chest with a thump in mock offense. "Are you saying that I'm not sexy as fuck? You just want me for my ginormous cock, don't you?"

Despite my cheeks heating and the eye rolls from some of the other patients, I wrapped my arms around his stomach and agreed that I only wanted him for his big dick.

"Next!" a voice shouted from behind the desk, alerting Rylan and me that it was our turn.

Quickly she checked us in and directed us to a seating area. The women there looked at me, a few turning their noses up in the air as I made eye contact. They were all in various stages of pregnancy. It was the first time I'd felt uncomfortable being an un-wed mother, even though I knew that strong women did it every day.

We waited for only a short time before a kind-looking nurse called our name and we were taken back to an ultrasound room. She instructed me to remove everything below the waist as this would be done with an internal wand instead of over the stomach.

I found myself laughing as Rylan's eyes visibly widened when he saw the nurse slip a cover on the instrument that would be used.

She left the room for a couple of minutes for me to undress and slip under the sheet. Rylan took a seat on the chair by the head of the bed.

"I can't believe they have to stick something up your. . .you know what."

"It's because the baby is so small that they will be able to detect it better that way."

"Whatever you say. All I know is it's killing me that you're naked under that flimsy sheet. I bet I could make you come before the nurse comes back." He lifted his eyebrows up and down suggestively.

Before I could respond, the nurse came back into the room, dimmed the lights, and sat at the machine.

"Do you have a full bladder?" she asked.

"Yes, ma'am."

"Good. That will make it easier to see the baby." The nurse looked at Rylan as she explained what I had been told on the phone when I made the appointment.

"I'm going to take a few measurements first, and then we'll verify if you're pregnant and how far along you are. Sound good?"

We both agreed and the nurse inserted the wand effortlessly. She'd done this a lot and knew what to do and say to put her patients at ease. Not even Rylan had questions.

After five minutes of measurements and pointing out my internal organs, she paused the wand. My eyes were glued to the screen and the black, white, and gray noise.

"There it is," she exclaimed, zooming in on an image projected on the television across from us. It displayed what showed on her machine screen. "That's your baby."

Was I an emotional person? Not at all, but I found a sob welling up as tears leaked from the corners of my eyes, watching the little nugget on the screen. Rylan's fingers wiped away the wetness as he pressed a soft kiss to the top of my head. At first thought, being a mom was absolutely terrifying. I was afraid of screwing up, of not being enough. But I knew that women did this every day.

"It looks like you're around ten weeks, as you had estimated. We'll go ahead and set your due date as November 2nd. Though that may change a little as we get closer."

She pressed a few buttons and pictures printed out, and then she handed them to us. I looked down at the images in complete awe. This was my baby growing inside of me. It made it real. I was going to be a mom.

"Congratulations. I'll let you get dressed and then take you back to see your doctor."

We thanked her, and soon enough, I was sitting in my regular doctor's office. Rylan and I hadn't had time to process everything as she handed me some pregnancy books and suggested that I start some prenatal vitamins.

When she asked if we had any questions, I silently shook my head. I was overwhelmed. All I wanted to do was stare at my baby's ultrasound picture.

"Actually, I have a question."

"Go ahead," Dr. Bowen replied.

"Is it okay to keep. . .you know. . .I mean. . ." Rylan made some gestures with his hand, and I rolled my eyes.

"Yes, it is perfectly safe for her to continue having intercourse. It's healthy even." I was sure that my face matched the color of Dr. Bowen's red lips. "Congratulations to both of you. You're going to be great parents. And I am certain that you'll have a beautiful and healthy baby."

We thanked her as we left her office and headed back to the car. Rylan had to guide me because my eyes were glued to the picture.

"Can you believe it?" I said with wonder. I had this tiny little human growing inside of me. Any reservations I'd had previously flew out the window.

We approached the car, but instead of opening the door, Rylan dropped to his knees. Gently he lifted my shirt, exposed my stomach, and pressed a soft kiss just below my navel.

"Thank you," he whispered as he gazed up at me.

"For what?" Absentmindedly I sank my fingers in his hair and brushed through the strands.

"For including me. For trusting me."

"This baby is half of you. Of course I want to involve you as much as you want to be. But, you may not be thanking me in a little bit."

"Why?"

"Because I thought we'd take my dad to lunch and tell him the news." My stoic Ridge Rogue visibly gulped as he stood. "Think of it like ripping off a band-aid."

"Except I die afterward."

"My father is not going to kill you." He huffed as he reached around me to open my door. Extending my arm, I gripped his wrist with my hand as he tried to shut the door. "Rylan, my dad will not kill you. He knows that you're important to me."

After ensuring I was secured in the seat, Rylan walked around the car with much less pep in his step than when we arrived. He took a heavy breath, settled in his seat, and then pulled out his phone.

"I guess you should make sure your dad is free for lunch. It looks like there is a Mexican place near his office."

Leaning over the center console, I brushed my lips against his cheek and thanked him. I messaged my dad, who happily agreed to meet us. Rylan and I had already figured out that we would miss classes this afternoon, so we were in no rush to return to campus.

Dad was waiting at the restaurant entrance when we arrived and the host took us back to a booth. I slid in first and Rylan took the seat beside me. Before anyone spoke, I took in the area around us. It was empty for the most part and I wasn't sure if that was a good or bad thing. If there were people around, my father would be less likely to yell and make a scene, not that my father had ever raised his voice at me. I was a good kid for the most part.

My fingers started tapping wildly on my leg. Rylan noticed the motion, set his hand on top of mine, and linked our fingers together.

"Well, this is a nice surprise," my dad said as he settled in his seat. "It's good to see you, Rylan. I never once believed that you and my Haley were just friends, by the way." He was trying to joke and Rylan chuckled like a good sport. I wondered if his heart was racing like mine and the lunch had been my idea.

On the way to the restaurant, I kept debating how I would break the news to my father. Should I ease him into the conversation? Should I wait until we were all done so I could make a quick run for it? But I never expected to blurt it out the moment we sat down.

"I'm pregnant." I slapped my hand over my mouth, and my eyes widened in alarm. I really needed to get a pregnancy filter. I never had the problem before.

The server chose that moment to bring over a few glasses of water and a basket of chips with a bowl of salsa. The sight of the food made my stomach roll. My father reached for his drink and took a hefty sip.

"I'm sorry. Tell me that again," he said.

"I'm. . .well, Rylan and I-" I began, but my nerves were getting the best of me. Rylan quickly took over with an ease I didn't know he possessed. "Dr. Sinclair, Haley and I are expecting. The baby is due in early November. Would you like to see a picture?"

I wasn't sure if my father was still trying to process what we'd said or if Rylan had completely mystified him, but my dad nodded his head without a word and accepted the long trail of images. When the server came back to ask if we wanted to order, Rylan must have asked if he could come back in a few minutes. The only sound I heard was the pounding of my heart in my ears. Come to think of it, the sound had a nice beat.

My dad stared down at the images Rylan had handed him. Disappointing my father was one of my biggest fears. He'd gone through so much already with Senator Hastings and my mom that I didn't want to be one more burden for him.

"Wow. I. . .I wish your mom was here. She always spoke about being a grandma one day. She couldn't wait."

I blinked quickly. This was not the reaction I had expected. I didn't think he'd throw a fit, but I imagined him reprimanding me in some way.

"You look surprised," my father added. "You're not a fifteen-year-old girl, Haley. You're a young woman that graduates college in a month. Hell, I was engaged to your mom at your age. We had you not shortly after.

"You're smart and have a good head on your shoulders. I'm here when you need me, but I have faith in you and Rylan." My father turned his pointed gaze on my seatmate. "I assume you plan on being in the picture, correct?"

"Yes, sir. I want to be there for everything."

"That's good to hear, son. Have either of you made plans after graduation?"

Rylan launched into a conversation about his internship and hopes for job prospects, making sure to mention that his brother and his fiancée had ensured him that he would have a spot with their wildlife sanctuary if Rylan needed time to sort through job prospects. Jolee's sanctuary had already received enough grants to fund the site's construction and employ a full staff for the next five years. She had already locked in investors for the next ten years as well. She really was exceptional when she had a goal in mind and this was all done in the last month.

I was glad that the most important guys in my life were getting along. It made whatever decisions Rylan and I made with the baby so much easier. That support system would be there.

Dad and Rylan seemed to have forged a new friendship by the time we finished lunch, which boded well for the baby and me.

"Have you thought about your living arrangements after graduation?"

"No, I haven't, but I thought about looking for a starter home between here and Wellington, so we're in driving distance to both grandparents."

"How did your family react, Rylan?"

"Well, you're the first to know, officially, but I'm certain Tracy will be excited. I'm sure she figured Link or Ford would be first to give her a grandchild since they're the oldest." When Rylan had joined me for dinner when Dad introduced Gina, he had explained to them that he had been adopted by Dr. Fincher at the age of twelve and had five other adopted brothers.

"Do you think you'll try to reach out to your birth parents?"

"No, sir. If they could abandon me in the hospital when I was nine, then they don't deserve any right to know their grandchild or me."

"I can't argue with you there and I'm sorry if I brought up any bad memories."

"Thank you, but I'm okay. I just prefer not to think about them. Especially knowing that I have my own child on the way, I can't comprehend how two people could just turn their back on their child or hurt them in some manner."

I'd never given much thought to Rylan's birth parents. He rarely spoke about them. I'd lucked out with mine. I could see that it was a touchy subject with him and it wasn't hard to imagine that their desertion was the factor that shaped Rylan's outlook on relationships. No one's leaving could hurt as bad when you didn't let them get close.

"Well, I need to get back to perfecting some smiles. This was a nice surprise, even more so with the baby news." We stood from the booth and my dad immediately held his arms out for me to fall into his embrace. I'd always loved his hugs, they reminded me of my childhood. "Keep me up to date on your appointments, please, and start to think about where you'd like to go for dinner after your graduation ceremony next month.

"Rylan, it was good to see you."

"You too, sir."

We walked out of the restaurant, but before we parted ways, I gave my dad one last hug and then watched as he walked down the sidewalk back to his practice.

"Your dad is really great."

"Yes, he is. I got really lucky in the family department."

We got settled in the car, and I decided that we needed to lay all the cards on the table. After all, I had told him about everything my dad and mom had gone through.

"Speaking of families. I think maybe it's time you share the backstory with yours."

"Haley," he warned.

"Please."

CHAPTER FOURTEEN
RYLAN

I'd expected this conversation to happen sometime, but I always diverted to another topic whenever there was an appropriate opening.

"Can it wait until we get back to your apartment?"

"As long as you promise not to try and distract me."

"Can I fuck you afterward?"

"We'll see."

The remainder of the car ride was done in silence. Haley scrolled through her phone looking for homes in the area. She bounced in her seat whenever she found one that she liked. Haley mentioned that she wanted to look for a realtor when we got back to campus.

I wasn't sure if we would officially call ourselves a couple, neither of us was big on labels, but with the baby on the way, we had breached a new level in our relationship. And if she wanted us to move in together, I was all for it.

When I thought of the future, it was usually filled with being the favorite uncle and a life of solitude, but since Haley came into my life, I never saw anything without her in it. Now she was going to be tied to me forever.

It terrified me to talk about my past. The proverbial knife wounds in my heart still felt as fresh as they had when I was nine.

"Do you want a beer?" Haley asked me as we entered her apartment. I felt bad for drinking alcohol when she couldn't, but I needed the liquid courage. I moved toward the couch as she went into the kitchen. It didn't take long before she joined me with the top popped on a local beer that I favored. I loved that she paid attention to things like that.

Haley waited patiently for me; the sound of our breathing filled the space. I finished the beer and knew that I'd waited long enough.

"It's not as bad as I make it out to be, but it kind of defines why I am the way that I am. The rape on top of this baggage didn't do me any favors either."

"I understand." Of course she did. Haley was so fucking understanding about everything. It was almost both a blessing and a curse for any relationship we may have. She'd probably brush it all aside if I ever treated her like my parents treated me. And she didn't deserve that.

"My birth parents were like rockstar hippies if that makes sense. They were in a band that did semi-well, but no record deals or anything. They played a lot of the Sex Pistols, if I remember correctly. Hell, apparently, that's how they gave me my last name. Sid Vicious' last name was Ritchie.

"Anyway, they never married and were not thrilled to have an unwanted pregnancy. Alice, my birth mom, never made it a secret that she'd try to abort me, but it failed or she missed the appointment window. Something like that. She even had Frankie, my birth father, push her down the stairs when she was nine months along.

"So, you can imagine growing up in an environment filled with drugs, sex, rock and roll, and your parents never caring or loving you. I think they even tried to sell me at some point or give me away. I don't know why they weren't successful.

RENEE HARLESS

"We lived out of their van, so I had to go everywhere with them. Any schooling I got was done by going to the library. When I was nine, they were playing a show at some club. When they played the bigger venues, I loved to climb up on the catwalks or balconies to stay as far away from them as I could. Most of the time, they never even knew that I was there. I grew to despise the music, but I wanted to be with them. I loved them.

"This one club was one of the biggest they'd been to. I was actually proud of them, and I'd hoped to get to watch them perform. This club had a catwalk above the stage, I guess for lights or something, but one of the grates wasn't secured, and I fell through. It was pretty high in the air; I don't know the exact measurement. One of the bass players for another band found me and called the ambulance. He said he'd make sure my parents came to the hospital.

"I remember being so scared when I got to the hospital and there was no one there to comfort me. There was no feeling below my neck and the surgeon was afraid I was paralyzed. They put me in a full-body cast just to be safe.

"The nurse said I kept asking for my mom and dad, but no one had shown up. I spent three months in the hospital without my parents coming to claim me.

Thank goodness I'd only broken my collarbone, arm, and leg. I can't imagine what I would have done had I been paralyzed."

"Oh, Rylan," Haley cried, tears streaming down her cheeks as she rested her hands gently over her stomach. I wasn't even sure if she knew she'd done it. Two months pregnant and she was already protecting our child.

Wishing that I had another beer, I cleared my throat and continued. "That's not even all of it. When the hospital was ready to discharge me, they learned that I'd never been issued a birth certificate or social security number. I literally didn't even exist.

"Social services ushered me around foster homes, and you know that dreaded story, but it wasn't until I came to be with Tracy that any of them cared enough to have all of the proper paperwork filed. If anything, I was lucky that my birth mother loved to celebrate birthdays, so I had that information, but nothing else. I don't even know the city where I was born.

"And, yeah, that's it."

Haley sat crying quietly, her face pressed against my shoulder as she tried to share the weight of my burdens. Ten minutes passed before she calmed.

"And you don't do relationships because you're afraid you're like your parents. . ."

"Pretty much. I've never been around any happy, functioning couples or family. Except for Tracy, your dad, and my brothers."

"Exactly. You have such a good and healthy relationship with them. You have to know that you're capable of more than what your birth parents provided. They're awful people, but you're not. Are they the reason you hate music too?"

"Yeah, but I love when you play if you hadn't figured it out."

"Well, then I'll have to play for you more often."

The conversation left me feeling like old wounds had been reopened and left to bleed out. I leaned back against the couch, tilted my head and closed my eyes. Haley pressed her body against mine, snuggling her smaller figure into a ball under my arm. Her head rested on my chest and I wondered if she could hear my heartbeat speed up.

"Thank you for sharing all of that with me."

"You're welcome. It feels good to tell someone."

After the weight of my story dissipated and my racing heart calmed, I asked Haley, "Do you regret sleeping with me. . .now that you're pregnant? Your entire life is changing because of me."

"It was my choice to have sex with you, Rylan. I understood the possible consequences."

"Still, you could have, I don't know. . ."

In a flash, Haley jumped from the couch and stood defiantly in front of me, hands on her curvy hips. Talk about a change in mood. "I could have what? Slept with someone else? Got pregnant by someone else?"

I stood from the couch and went toe to toe with her. The tips of our noses touched as I leaned over her because she barely hit my chest in heels. "Hell no. The moment you asked me to fuck you in Spain you were mine, cat. Do you understand? You're fucking mine and no one else can have you. And you better fucking believe any kids you have will be mine."

I was breathing hard enough that I struggled to pull enough air into my lungs. My fists clenched at my side, while Haley stood before me in all her radiant beauty with a wide smile on her lips.

"I love you too, Rylan," she whispered as she lifted her arms to wrap around my neck, her fingers diving into the strands of hair at the base of my head.

"I never said. . .Ah, fuck." How the hell did she figure it out before I did?

"It's okay. Everything will work out."

I reached around her body and tugged her closer, pressing my lips to her forehead in a soft kiss before I tucked her head under my chin. "God, I fucking love you, Hales, and that terrifies me."

"You're not your parents, Ry. You're so much better than them."

"So now that I've declared that you're mine, I want to take you back to your bedroom and feel you ride my cock until we can't remember our names."

A couple of hours later, I woke to a naked Haley lying on top of me. The room was dark and the sun had fallen beyond the horizon hours ago. The lamp in the entryway was on and left the hall in a warm glow. Haley usually slept with her bedroom door closed, but we'd spent three hours testing how many orgasms we could have.

The doctor mentioned that she could be uncomfortable sleeping on her stomach. I slipped free from under her arm, praying that she didn't wake up, and made sure that I turned her onto her side. I searched the floor for my shorts, tugged them on, and exited the room, closing the door behind me.

Once I reached the living room, I heard the remnants of someone's party and wondered if Link was home. I wanted to talk to him about everything going on, but there was no chance in hell I was going to risk Haley waking up and finding me gone again. It kills me to think that I almost lost her that night. I planned on never making that mistake again.

And I really needed to deal with the guys from my classes. They kept threatening to call me out on the deal they made when we were studying abroad, though I made it clear I wasn't interested in their "investment". Those lying scumbags were going to wind up in jail before they turned thirty. I hung out with them, for lack of a better word, because they were teaching me the kind of sleazeballs to stay away from when I graduated. I also didn't want them going behind my back. The whole mentality of keeping your enemies closer rang true in this case.

My phone was where I left it on the coffee table and I grabbed it, opening the contacts to Link's name.

Me: Hey, you home?

Link: Yeah

Me: I'm down at Haley's. Meet me?

He didn't reply and I never expected him to. Not five seconds later, there was a knock on the door and I let Link inside with a beer at the ready for him.

"Nice, thanks," he said as he accepted the drink and followed me to Haley's couch. "What's on your mind? I figured you didn't invite me here to chill and play video games."

I sat next to him on the couch and sipped my own beer.

Turning to face him, I said, "Haley's pregnant."

"Oh, wow. Okay, that was not what I was expecting you to say." Link took a large gulp of his beer before placing the bottle on the coffee table.

"We used protection, but obviously, I have super sperm or something."

"Or something. You tell Mom yet?"

"Not yet. Haley's told the girls, and we told her dad today. Oh," I exclaimed as I stood up and pulled the folded images from my back pocket and handed the ultrasound pictures to him. "This is the baby. The due date is early November."

Link stayed quiet for a while as he stared at the pictures. There really wasn't much to see, just some black and gray and a little peanut-looking thing in the middle.

"Congratulations, Ry," he said as he casually draped his arm around me and tugged me into a casual hug. "You're going to be a great dad."

"You think?"

"Absolutely. You always put everyone's needs above your own. You listen when someone is speaking. And you have a big heart, Rylan. I knew that when you came to live with us."

"I told her. Everything, she knows everything." Link and Tracy were the only people that knew my entire history. Link was one of those people that you met and immediately gave your backstory. He had that way about him. That was probably why he was in school to get his doctorate and become a counselor.

"Good. That's a big step for you."

Link and I chatted a bit longer. Mainly, he helped me settle my fears about becoming a father. He asked if Haley and I would tie the knot before the baby came, and though we hadn't discussed it, I was sure Haley would want to wait a while. We hadn't been together long enough for a commitment like that. Hell, it took her calling me out to realize that I was in love with her.

Link left an hour later. I returned to the bedroom, dropped my shorts, and curled myself around Haley. I was wide awake but more than content to watch her sleep. Gently I placed my hand on her stomach and thought about the fact she was growing a life inside her body. A little boy or girl that would call us Mom and Dad. And I silently made a vow that I would never abandon my kid the way I had been.

Pressing my lips to Haley's head, I whispered, "I love you, cat," then joined her in sleep.

CHAPTER FIFTEEN
HALEY

I took Rylan to see so many homes in the last two weeks that it went from being fun to turning into a complete chore. I loathed whenever my realtor called me and I ignored her messages half of the time. It didn't help that she flirted with Rylan in front of me, though he never returned her affections. He was one hundred percent focused on me and what I wanted. I was the one with the hefty sum to spend on the house where I would bring my baby home.

I was being picky, but I was afraid to settle for just any old house. I wanted to walk inside and immediately know that the place was for me. Rylan was going to move in after graduation, but he kept his thoughts to himself when we went to showings. I wanted him to enjoy the place as much as I did.

"This is the last one for today," I told Rylan as we turned the corner to enter the neighborhood. I'd stopped showing him pictures of the listings because we'd learned too many times that the pictures could, and would, be deceiving.

"Okay. We're in no rush, Hales. We'll find you and nugget the perfect house. Although, I still wish you'd let me help."

After we told Tracy about the pregnancy, she was so overjoyed that she offered to pay the down payment on whatever house we found. It felt wrong to take the money from her, but she insisted every time we got together, which was at least every Sunday for dinner.

My dad was no different. He wanted to purchase a house for us as a graduation present. I was at the point where I was going to let them do whatever they wanted because the confrontations were driving me nuts. My hormones couldn't stand it.

"Can we get ice cream after this?" I asked Rylan as he turned onto the street where the house was located. I was nuts for ice cream. That seemed to be my only craving.

"Maybe? If you're a good girl."

In mock horror, I admonished him. "How dare you? I'm always a good girl."

"Well, can you be a bad girl then?" he asked suggestively as the house came into view.

It had been one of my favorites. A cape cod style with white siding and bright blue shutters. There were even cedar shingles lining the second story. It reminded me of a beach house.

"Wow," Rylan whispered as he parked the car in front of the attached garage.

I may have started this journey looking for a starter home, but if I could afford my forever home, there was nothing wrong with that either. This house was just slightly out of the price range I wanted to stay in, but it was everything I'd ever dreamed of. A perfectly manicured lawn on a full acre, which outside of Boston was not easy to come by, a swing set in the backyard, and five bedrooms.

Kate, our realtor, was parked on the street and most likely waiting inside. Rylan and I stepped out of the car and stared up at the house. I gazed over at him but I couldn't read his expression.

"Are you ready to go inside? Kate's here."

"No." His voice was strong and assured and I was completely taken aback.

"What? But this house is. . ."

"Perfect. I don't even need to go inside to know that this is the house, Haley. I felt it the minute we pulled up."

"Really?" I asked in wonder. We hadn't agreed on a property yet, but I instantly knew that this was the house for us.

"Yep."

"Well, can you at least humor me and look at the rooms. What if the previous owners destroyed the inside? What if the kitchen has green appliances?" I asked in mock horror.

"I'll go look inside for you, but this is it, cat. This is our house. This is where we'll raise our baby." Talk about melting on the spot. I was no better than an ice cream cone on a hot day.

Rylan came around the car and grabbed my hand, smiling down at me in a way that was a mix of happiness and desire. It was my favorite.

With Kate's guidance, we explored the house and I was happy to note that the interior was just as impeccable as the exterior. Our realtor left us to walk through the house once more by ourselves, where we ended up in the small bedroom on the second floor across from the master bedroom.

Together Rylan and I walked toward the window that overlooked the backyard and stood holding hands. I leaned my head on his shoulder and

Rylan released my hand, draping his arm over my shoulders to tug me closer.

"Want to go fuck in the master bathroom?" My laugh exploded in the room, but it was exactly the kind of mood breaker Rylan and I needed.

"We will definitely make sure to christen that room first."

"Promise?"

"One hundred percent. Now, let's go talk to Kate about putting in an offer. Oh my gosh, I'm so excited!" I said gleefully.

"It's already done."

"What?" I said as he grasped my hand again and led me downstairs where Kate was waiting in the kitchen.

"Is it everything you expected, Mr. Ritchie?" Kate asked as he approached.

"Yes, thank you. Is there anything else you need on our end?"

"Nope. I have submitted the offer and I suspect we'll hear back within the next twenty-four hours."

"Great. Thank you. And please remind them we'd like to move in sooner rather than later."

I had no idea what was going on. There was a conversation flowing around me and I felt like I was a witness from the outside, because I was.

"Can someone explain to me what's going on?" I asked as I dropped Rylan's hand and turned to face him, ignoring Kate's nervous gaze.

"Just remember that we love you." I stared at him not liking where the conversation was heading. "Your dad and Tracy came to me and asked if they, together, could pay the down payment on the house for us. We can talk about everything in detail later, but it's a baby gift to us from them."

"But it's so expensive, I can't ask them to-"

"You don't have to ask, cat. They want to do this for us, for you and me and the baby, because they love us."

There was no point in arguing because I did understand their desire to take care of us. We were their kids and they were in a situation where they could provide for us, even though we could do it on our own. I was afraid of hurting them if I continued to turn it down. Plus, we could easily house some of the family with the five bedrooms.

"There is one more thing, though. If the owners accept the offer, the house will be in your name. That was my requirement when I agreed to our parents' deal."

"But why?" It seemed ridiculous that his mom would help pay for the house, but his name wouldn't be on the title.

"Because this is the house where our child will grow up, their grandchild. They want what's best for all of us. We can easily fill out the paperwork to add my name if and when the time is right. But I never want you to feel like you have no place to go with our child. This house is yours. I'm here for as long as you'll let me be."

Forever is what I wanted to shout at him, but I understood his reservations. We had never given our relationship a title or name, and we'd only been intimate since December. Was four months long enough to know that you wanted to spend your life with someone?

"Okay," I'd whispered against the stubble on Rylan's cheek as I wrapped my arms around him in an embrace.

A sudden noise turned our attention to the front door, where Kate dashed inside.

"The offer has been accepted!" she shouted. "We can close in thirty days."

That would be the weekend before graduation; talk about excitement. I launched myself into Rylan's arms as he held me tightly against his body.

"God, I love you," I whispered against his mouth as I sealed our lips together. Rylan spun around and set me on the butcherblock countertop of the island as he kissed me in return. We didn't hear the sound of the door closing but Rylan soon pulled away and reminded me that I had my final rehearsal that evening for the spring performance. I hadn't wanted to leave the house, the place where I would watch our child grow. I was ready to grow up and move on with my life.

"Come on, cat. Once we get home, you can start picking out furniture for the place." If there were ever any way to convince me to leave the house, that would be it. "Plus, Kate's probably waiting for us to leave so she can close up," he joked.

****

We moved my things into the house the weekend before graduation. I couldn't believe that Rylan and I lived together in the space. He and I still never officially discussed our relationship status, it was just known that we were together. There were many females with broken hearts across campus.

For the first time, I was glad that I was curvier. It helped mask my pregnancy. Despite my hunger for ice cream, I had no other symptoms. The only time I was nauseated was when I skipped a meal.

My spring performance for the arts department also took place the same weekend that we moved. The furniture I ordered only had that time available. By the time I took the stage, I was exhausted, but the adrenaline of performing gave me the kick I needed for the two performances.

I'd expected Rylan and my dad to be in attendance, but I hadn't expected his entire family to show up to support me. Having the Ridge Rogues in the audience cheering me on was surreal. They all had flowers waiting for me after the show and though I wasn't big on attention, it felt nice that they'd recognized my hard work.

The graduation ceremony was outside and I was thankful for the cooler spring air in Boston. My row was near the back, and Rylan's was only about three rows ahead of mine. Every once in a while, he'd peer over his shoulder at me and wink.

The girl beside me leaned over and said, "Oh my gosh, I think one of the Rogues is looking back at me." I had to stifle my laugh. Rylan and I had been pretty certain that every female within a ten-mile radius of Wellington had heard he was taken off the market, but maybe a few had slipped through. But since it was graduation, I figured I'd let her continue living her fantasy.

"Maybe. He does keep looking this way." It wasn't an actual lie, just a stretching of the truth. And by the way her voice squeaked, she took me at my word. I waited to see if she'd start waving him down.

Glancing down at the program in my hand, I smirked when the small stone on my left hand caught the light. It was no engagement ring. We hadn't even spoken about the future after the baby was born. But the night of my performance, after Rylan had shown me just how much he enjoyed the show, he gave me a white gold band with a large amethyst stone in the center. When I began freaking out, he had to assure me, multiple times, that it was not a proposal; he'd just come to terms with being in love and in a relationship and wasn't ready for more than that. Neither was I.

He gave it to me because he wanted anyone who saw me, especially with the pregnancy, to know without a doubt that the baby and I were loved and not alone. The ring symbolized his promise to us that he would do everything he could to take care of us.

And he'd been worried that he was going to be awful at being in a relationship. So far, he had nailed it.

I wore the ring with pride and ignored the questions and stares that it tended to bring up in conversation.

The Dean called out Rylan's name and his family was loud and boisterous as he walked across the stage to accept his diploma. Alarming the students seated around me, I stood and cheered him on. They probably thought I was a nutjob, but I didn't care what they thought of me at that moment. I was proud of my man.

When I sat back down, the girl next to me stared with wide eyes.

"What?" I asked her, but she remained quiet.

Rylan winked in my direction as he returned to his seat and sat down.

"Oh my gosh, do you know each other?"

"He's my boyfriend." I tried not to sound smug at the confession, but it probably came out that way. Luckily I was saved from explaining further when our row was gestured to move toward the stage.

"Don't trip. Don't trip. Don't trip," I repeatedly mumbled until the announcer called my name.

"Haley Sinclair."

Taking a deep breath, I slowly took the stairs and made my way over to the Dean, where I shook his hand and then the hands of the department faculty. There were cheers from out in the audience, but I was too focused on not making a fool of myself. When my sandal touched the solid ground, I finally released my breath.

I waved at Rylan as I walked by his row before returning to my seat. He blew a kiss in my direction and I felt my heart skip a beat. Anytime he did something like that, the butterflies fluttered wildly in my stomach.

We'd already made plans to join our families separately after the ceremony since we were living together. There would be a special kind of celebration at home afterward — something involving some special lingerie I picked up the other day.

Once the last person returned to their seat, the Dean congratulated us all again. Then in a loud battle cry, the seniors stood and tossed their black caps in the air. Well, not me. I planned on keeping mine and it stayed bobby pinned in place. I noticed Rylan hadn't tossed his either, probably because he just didn't care, but he did remove it from his head. Students and family were moving all around, but I caught a glimpse of him running his hand through his dark hair. Whenever he did that, I was sure that I'd melt into a puddle of goo on the floor.

"I'm so proud of you, sweetie!" Strong arms wrapped around me from behind and I sank into my father's hug.

"Thank you, Dad. Gina! I'm so glad you could make it." Gina held her arms out for an embrace and I returned it. She and my dad were so happy together and I had a suspicion that Dad may propose to her soon. It seemed like relational next steps were on the horizon for all the Sinclairs.

"Are you ready for lunch? I made reservations at the seafood place you love so much."

"Thanks. Yeah, I just want to say goodbye to Rylan really quick. I'll meet you at the car?"

"Sure, we're parked just outside the library."

Standing on my tiptoes, I pressed a kiss to my dad's cheek and thanked him.

I unzipped my black graduation gown as I made my way to where I'd seen Rylan standing with his family. The group was no longer there but I caught sight of him near the front of the stage. I could always pick him out in a crowd.

Unfortunately, as I got closer, I noticed that the guys from his department that had traveled abroad were surrounding him. They made my stomach crawl and my flight instincts kicked into gear.

"Ah, look, the little wifey came to save the day," one of them snickered as they caught sight of me. They'd all looked like they had been drinking. I wouldn't have been surprised. "She must be a good lay for you to stick around this long."

"Shut the fuck up, dude." Rylan shoved the guy, who fell into one of the others.

"Think I can have a turn? I'll let you keep your money. Hell, for breaking her in, I'll even give you a grand."

My body felt chilled to the bone despite the warm air. They couldn't have been talking about me. There was no way that they had the audacity to ask if they could sleep with me.

"Excuse me?" I asked, fearing the salacious leer the five men gave me. The most hurtful was the shame in Rylan's gaze.

"Oh, we were sure Rylan here would have told you that we were going to give five grand to whoever could sleep with you first. None of us expected it would take the entire fucking semester for it to happen."

My throat began to close up and I couldn't breathe. There was no way this was happening to me.

They'd bet on having sex with me. That was only something you'd see in the movies, not in real life. Not in my life.

"So, you what? Made a bet to sleep with me? Is that it?" I pointed the question at Rylan, but one of the other assholes spoke instead.

"Pretty much. You were the weird chick with the big rack that wouldn't give any of us the time of day. Kept us busy during the semester."

I wanted to go over and slap them all. I wanted to take away the one thing that seemed to contain their brains – their tiny penises. How could they treat anyone like this and this that it was okay?

"Is it true, Rylan?"

He looked at me, his eyes wide and scared and I knew the answer before he even replied. It didn't matter that I knew he'd catch up to me. I turned around and dashed across the field. I needed to be away from all the people who watched the exchange.

"Haley!" Rylan called out to me, his voice cracking with emotion. It broke my heart a little because all the good he gave me was built on a bet. "Haley, please," he repeated.

A hand landed on my elbow and spun me around. I was already lightheaded from the sun, so my vision went a little off-kilter.

"I swear to you, Haley, you were not part of a bet for me. I told them I didn't want any part of it."

"I. . .I don't want to hear it right now, okay? You had every chance in the world to tell me before now. But those fucking creeps had to be the ones to tell me. God, why are you even friends with them? It's like I don't know you at all."

Jerking my arm from his grasp, I took a step away, and then another, leaving a devastated Rylan staring at me. But what did he have to be devastated about? My virginity was bought for five thousand dollars.

"Please, Haley, I love you. After everything, you have to know that. You have to know that."

I did know that he loved me. He made sure I knew it every day, but the duplicity felt like an iron fist squeezing the air from my lungs.

"I. . .I need to go," I said, inching away from him. "I need some time."

A crowd had formed around us because everything one of the Ridge Rogues did was interesting. Thankfully they parted as I walked away.

Somehow I made it to the parking lot where my father and Gina were waiting. They were so excited about graduation that I didn't have the heart to tell them that I was breaking inside. But by the time lunch was over, I told them that Rylan and I had fought, but I didn't disclose the details. I wasn't sure Rylan would live to see another day if he knew that some stupid kids made a bet to sleep with me.

Dad encouraged me to talk to him, but Gina must have sensed that there was more to the story and insisted that I take all of the time I needed.

When it came time to leave, I couldn't even imagine going back to the house I was supposed to share with him. The house I grew up in was already sold, and while I knew that I could ask my dad or my friends if I could crash at their places, I didn't want to have to explain any of the details.

I rode back to Gina's house and called for a car service with plans to stay at a hotel in Boston for a couple of nights. Room service and a couple of nights alone would be good for me. I couldn't ignore Rylan forever, but I needed to let my heart mend a little first.

"Are you sure, sweetie?" my dad asked as he walked with me to meet the rideshare.

"Yeah. I just need some alone time, I think. Just a couple of days."

"Okay, just be careful and text me your room number when you get there."

"I will. I love you, Daddy."

"I love you too. I'm sorry your day didn't turn out as good as you imagined."

"That's okay. Luck has never really been on my side anyway."

We hugged, my dad squeezing a bit tighter before allowing me to settle into the car. Turning around on my seat, I watched Dad shrink in size as the car pulled farther away from Gina's house. He had finally found happiness again and deserved it more than anyone I knew.

But when would it be my turn?

CHAPTER SIXTEEN
RYLAN

It had been three days since I'd seen or spoken to Haley and I was going mad. I couldn't sleep, couldn't eat. Hell, I'd barely showered since Link found me drunk in the house I was supposed to share with Haley the night after the graduation ceremony. Somehow I had managed to make it to lunch with Mom and my brothers, but everything after that was a blur. I'd been staying at my mom's place since that night. I couldn't bear to be around Haley's things knowing that I may have lost her.

I was a wreck. All I wanted was to explain everything to Haley. I know that it seemed bad, and it was, but she had to know that I told those fuckers that they were morons when they made that bet and that I'd never acknowledged it. I was with her because I wanted to be, not because I wanted the money or to prove myself to them. God, it killed me knowing that I hurt her.

Somehow in my drunken stupor, I'd confessed to Link and Ford everything that'd happened. They had sided with her, of course. I had not done anything wrong, just kept the truth about the dickheads in my class.

I was slated to start my internship on Monday, but I was so emotionally drained I was afraid I wouldn't make it. I needed to, though. A lot was riding on it for the university and me.

Grabbing my phone, I sent another message to Haley, just as I had been every hour for the last three days.

"Rylan. Can you come down here, please?" Mom beckoned.

She was worried about me, I could see it in her eyes every day, and I had a feeling she was going to force me to eat something.

When I descended the stairs, Mom was waiting with a soft smile.

"Hey. It's such a pretty day outside. I thought it would be nice to take a walk. What do you say?"

"Mom, I'm not sure that's a good idea."

"Well, I do. I also sent Link to check on Haley. A little birdie told me that she was stopping by the house today, and even though I know you want to rush over there, she may be more willing to talk to him first."

The desire to rush out the door, grab a car, and make my way to the house was so high I almost couldn't think straight, but Mom's hand on my arm kept me grounded in place.

"I promise you, Rylan, everything is going to work out as it's meant to. I know you don't want to discuss anything, and I can only guess that whatever happened was big. You need to give her time for you and the baby. And you need to come to terms with the fact that she may decide she's better without you. That is a consequence you may have to face. But if I know you and that big heart you have, you will find a way to make it all work out. Just let her be for a little while.

"Now, join me for a walk? The fresh air could do you some good."

"Can I take a quick shower first?"

Mom laughed and said she thought she'd smelled something that reminded her of a teenage boy. I quickly ran upstairs, chucked my clothes off in the bedroom I had been occupying, and then jumped in the shower. I didn't even bother adjusting the temperature of the spray; the cold water would help wake me up from this fog I'd been in.

Quickly I put on some clean clothes and shoved my phone in my back pocket before making my way downstairs to join Tracy. I found her in the kitchen with her phone pressed to her ear and a somber expression on her face.

I gave her a questioning look and heard her say that we'd be right there. I didn't need to ask to know that something was wrong. I'd only seen that look of grief when she told us Dad had died.

"Mom?"

She didn't hesitate. "Link was parked across the street and saw Haley pull up. He said she didn't look good. Paler than normal and like she hadn't been sleeping. He thinks that it would be best if you went over there. Link didn't feel that was his place."

Without a second thought, I grabbed Mom's keys off the little desk in the kitchen and motioned for her to join me. The drive to my house took twenty minutes, but I made it in ten. Different scenarios ran through my mind the entire time, and I knew until I pulled up and found everything okay, I was going to worry.

The car skidded as I pulled into the driveway, not even bothering to turn off the ignition. In the distance, I heard Mom call out that she and Link would be right behind me.

"Haley!" I shouted as I entered the house, letting the screen door slam behind me. "Haley!" I cried out again with no answer. The house was silent apart from the noise outdoors encroaching through the screen door.

Chills ran down my spine as I dashed through the first floor with no sign of Haley. I could only hope that maybe she was upstairs in the shower and couldn't hear me.

I called out her name again as I ran up the stairs, checking our master bedroom first but finding it empty.

"Rylan?" I heard my mom call as she entered the house. I was too busy searching for Haley to acknowledge her.

Stepping into the room we had decided would be the nursery, my heart dropped to the floor. My girl was sitting in the rocking chair we'd picked out with her head resting against her shoulder, completely unconscious.

I rushed over and called out her name, even lightly tapped her cheeks, but she wasn't responding. Link was right. She was much paler than normal, with dark purple coloring under her eyes.

"Mom, call 911. Haley is unconscious," I cried out as I lifted her in my arms. It was already scary to see her sitting so lifeless, but as I picked her up, I noticed the stain of blood on the ivory seat cushion.

"Oh, God. She's bleeding. Mom! Link! She's bleeding.

"Oh, baby. Please wake up," I pleaded with her as I carefully carried her down the stairs trying not to jostle her.

Mom fussed about as we waited for the ambulance to arrive. They said they were two minutes out, but it felt like a lifetime. All I could imagine was that I had lost my girl and now I was losing the baby too.

If I was crying, no one said anything, but everything around me was a blur as I sat on the front steps with Haley cradled in my arms. I pressed my face into her hair, the smell of lavender and vanilla felt like home in this moment of anguish.

I didn't remember the paramedics arriving or that I fought one of them when they tried to take Haley from my arms. The ride in the ambulance was a fury of stats and hooking Haley up to machines. I felt helpless, but one of the EMTs assured me that simply holding Haley's hand and speaking to her could do better than medicines sometimes. So that's what I did. I spoke about all of the things we were going to do until we turned ninety.

Eventually, we arrived at the hospital and they wheeled her out of the ambulance and I was directed to the waiting area. I hated hospitals and felt more alone now than when I was abandoned at nine.

It took only a few minutes for Mom and Link to arrive, joining me in the waiting room. My brothers were going to come soon with Haley's friends; Link had called them on the way.

I wasn't sure how long I'd been sitting in the crappy chair holding Mom's hand, but she never wavered in sharing her strength with me.

"Oh, God!" I said as I stood abruptly, startling my family, who had taken the available seats around me. "I need to call her dad. Fuck."

Grabbing my phone, I looked down at the time and noticed it had been a full hour since we arrived.

From beside me, a gentle voice spoke up. "I called him when we arrived. I'm sorry if that wasn't my place, but I figured you were probably overwhelmed in worrying about Haley."

Slowly I sat back down and thanked Jolee for calling Dr. Sinclair. I wasn't sure I could share this kind of news with him.

"He was on his way when he messaged me thirty minutes ago," she added.

It wasn't much longer before a commotion sounded from the reception desk where Dr. Sinclair was asking for his daughter. On shaky legs, I stood and made my way over to him. I was afraid he would yell and blame me for his daughter being in the hospital. I'd been blaming myself since I found her in the nursery.

He followed me to the waiting area my family had filled and took a seat on the other side of Tracy. I explained what happened and how I found her and he visibly paled and shook as he took a breath.

"The family of Haley Sinclair?" a nurse called just as Daniel had settled. The group of us stood, and the nurse's eyes widened in surprise as she took in all of us.

Daniel took a few steps forward and I followed suit.

"I'm her father," he said and gestured to me. "And this is her fiancé and the father of the baby." My eyes darted over to him when he called me her fiancé and I was both surprised and relieved. I was afraid that the hospital was going to keep me from seeing her. Dr. Sinclair solved the issue without me even asking.

"Okay, follow me, please," the nurse replied. She directed us to a room and then said the doctor would be right in.

"You can go in first. I'll wait here," I told Daniel, still waiting for him to place the blame on me, but it never came. Instead, he grabbed my arm and tugged me into the room with him.

I looked up at the ceiling, not ready to see Haley in a worse state than the one I'd found her in. That image would be forever etched in my mind. If I ever thought the abandonment of my parents was life-changing, losing Haley was the end of everything.

"Dad?" her husky voice questioned and I felt my eyes well, my entire body trembling as I realized she was alive.

"Hey, sweetie."

He dropped my arm and I used my thumb and pointer finger to press against my closed eyelids to hold back the tears.

"Rylan," she called out, her voice mixed with awe and surprise. I'd never heard anything as beautiful. Shuffling in place, I moved my gaze from the ceiling and focused on her for the first time. She looked. . .good. Healthy. Nothing like the dying girl I held in my arms an hour ago.

"They said you were the one that brought me in." She held her hand out to me and I instantly moved across the room and latched onto her.

"Yeah. I went to check on you after everything and I found you." I swallowed hard as I added on that I'd lost ten years of my life when I saw her there.

The door to the room opened, but I couldn't look away from Haley and it seemed she felt the same; her gaze never pulled from mine.

"Ms. Sinclair. I'm glad to see you're awake and doing so well. We want to get one more bag of fluids in you and then you should be good to go. We'll send you home with a prescription for an iron supplement as well."

"Can you tell us what happened?"

Haley finally pulled her eyes away and nodded at the doctor, who went on to tell us that she came in severely dehydrated, which caused the cramping and bleeding. Haley was also severely low on iron, which caused her to faint.

"Is the baby okay?" I whispered, shifting my eyes down to Haley's stomach. She'd just started showing the tiniest of baby bumps.

"Yes, the baby is safe and healthy. We can bring in the ultrasound machine if you want to see it yourself."

"Yes, please," Haley and I said at the same time, both of us laughing.

The doctor left to get the machine and Haley's father said he would go inform our family and friends while we spent some time together.

Before he left, Daniel called out my name and said, "Rylan, you did good, son. I'll never be able to repay you."

Well, shit.

When we were alone, Haley and I grew quiet. I wasn't sure what to say. I'd sent her dozens of messages explaining everything in the last three days since she wouldn't take my calls, but I had no idea if she'd actually read them.

"I got your messages."

"Oh." My heart sank.

"I'm sorry I didn't reply. I. . .I didn't quite know what to say."

"I'm sorry, Haley. You have to know that."

"I do. I believe you," she replied as she patted the bed beside her hip so that I could sit down. God, her eyes looked like such a bright purple, I couldn't get enough of them.

"I never took the bet with them. I told them they could shove their five thousand up their asses. It's why I joined you at the bar. I didn't want any of them to try and drug you or something worse. But I knew the moment I approached you, they would believe that I was game.

"I'll never forgive myself for not telling you then what they were doing. The only explanation I have is that it was nice to enjoy a moment with just you. No classmates, no friends, no brothers, just us."

She remained quiet for a moment as I reached out and stroked her hair. It gave me a bit of hope when she leaned into my touch.

"Thank you for explaining. I had plans to see you today. It's why I went to the house. I missed you and I was ready to hear your side of the story. It was stupid of me to walk away without listening to you. I blame the hormones," she told me with a small laugh.

"When did you start feeling bad?"

"During graduation. I thought it was just the sun getting to me. I cried a lot in the hotel where I was staying and I didn't drink much water while I was there. I'm going to assume that was the cause of all of this."

A knock sounded on the door as a nurse walked in, wheeling a machine behind her. Wordlessly she plugged things into the wall and squirted some gel on a wand.

"Ready to see your little one?" she joyfully asked.

"Yes," Haley and I said in unison.

I stood and moved to the head of the bed, dropping a quick kiss on Haley's lips as I moved out of the nurse's way. She asked Haley to lift her gown as she tucked the blankets around Haley's waist. The wand moved around Haley's waist and then the room filled with a whoosh-whoosh sound.

"There's your baby moving around. Do you know the gender yet?" she asked us, our eyes fixed on the screen.

"No, not yet," I answered.

"Would you like to?" Haley and I exchanged glances before we eagerly agreed.

"Well, Mom and Dad, I'm happy to tell you that you're having a healthy baby boy. Congratulations."

"Oh, wow," I whispered as the nurse pointed out the heart and spine to Haley, but I was still stuck on the fact that we were having a little boy.

Not long after the nurse left, another entered the room with Haley's discharge papers and a wheelchair. Haley's clothes were placed in a bag and she was given a set of scrubs to wear home.

She hated that I had to wheel her out of the room, but her shame was quickly replaced with joy when she saw all of her friends waiting for her. I stood back with her dad as they all bent to hug her. Even my brothers took the time to make sure she was feeling better.

"Actually, we have some exciting news," I said once everyone had a chance to speak to Haley. I waited for her to give me the go-ahead. "We're having a boy."

By the sound our families and friends made in the waiting room you'd thought we'd won millions of dollars. They hugged each other and made jokes about how they were going to spoil him.

Leaning down, I whispered in Haley's ear, "You ready to go home?"

"Yes. Let's go home."

***

"Haley," I called out as I placed the burgers on the grill. "Can you bring me the slices of cheese?"

It was the end of summer and we were hosting a barbeque for the family at our house. We'd finally finished decorating and filling the rooms with furniture. Haley gave it a modern bohemian vibe that immediately relaxed me anytime I walked in the door.

I'd finished my internship last week, which meant I officially graduated. The business director I'd worked with had offered me a position, but I turned it down. After turning in my notes for the university about the business side of running a music therapy program, Dr. Caldwell contacted me about a position. It seemed that one of his colleagues owned a business consulting company and Dr. Caldwell had shared that he was impressed with my notes. I went for an interview a month ago and they brought me on as a junior consultant. I was starting next week.

Haley was still trying to figure out what she wanted to do, but I found her searching on the internet about music therapy programs. She'd shown a lot of interest in the program where I was interning. I had a feeling that if she decided to do something after the baby was born, it would be to go back to school.

"Here you go," Haley said as she handed me a pack of cheese before pressing a kiss to my cheek. She tried to slip away, but I snaked my arm around her waist and held her tight against me, leaning down and brushing my lips against her mouth.

"Thanks, cat."

We'd come a long way in a couple of months and we had a long way to go, but I knew Haley and I were going to get there. Not only were we determined to make a good life for our child, but we loved each other fiercely. It just took some mistakes to realize.

I gazed out at the yard. My brothers were wrestling like kids. Their girls were huddled in chairs around the unlit fire pit. Our parents were sitting at the table on the patio. I had never envisioned a setting like this for myself.

I almost wished that I could show my parents what I'd done with my life. The kid they left behind like he was a nobody. The kid that put their trust in people that took everything from him. The kid that never knew what the next day was going to bring.

I knew I had everything I would ever need with Haley tucked under my arm. And the baby was going to be the icing on the cake.

"This is nice." I smiled down at Haley as she sighed softly.

"This is everything."

EPILOGUE
RYLAN

"Where is everyone?" Haley asked as I came down the stairs. "Gabe is going to wake from his nap in a few minutes."

Because it was our first Christmas in the house, the family was coming for Christmas dinner. Haley was a little freaked out cooking for everyone, even though I kept trying to tell her that none of my family cared about the food. She didn't believe me.

She stood at the sink and I pressed my body against her back. I knew one surefire way to calm Haley down. I palmed my way under her shirt until I reached her breasts. Haley was breastfeeding Gabe, so I knew that they were full and ultra-sensitive.

"Rylan," she moaned as she arched her back, pushing her breasts against my hands.

Leaning down, I pressed my lips to her neck exposed by her black sweater. I trailed kisses up until I reached her jawline.

"Kiss me, cat."

She turned in my arms, and despite that I hated losing the feel of her chest, I was easily drunk on her kiss. We still hadn't been given the approval for sex since Gabe arrived two weeks late. Haley had her six-week appointment next Monday and we were both ready to get the go-ahead. But I never tired of feasting on her pussy.

"Distract me?" she asked as she kneeled down, unzipping my fly as she went.

"Ah, fuck," I whimpered as she pulled my cock free of my boxers and swiped her tongue across the tip. The feeling left my thighs shaking and I needed to brace my hands against the dark granite counters.

Haley wrapped her hand around the base of my shaft as she covered my tip with her mouth.

"That's it, cat. I want to fuck your mouth until you gag. Take all of it, baby."

She looked glorious as she worked my cock with her mouth and hand. The sounds coming from her mouth had my cock doubling in size.

"Babe, yeah. Just like that. Let me feel the back of your throat. Fuck." I could feel my orgasm spiraling higher until I had to mumble that I was coming. I gripped her hair as I held her still and released my cum down the back of her throat.

"My God, you're so fucking good at that," I told her as I slipped free from her mouth. She gazed up at me with her purple eyes that still mesmerized me.

Before I had a chance to return the favor, the baby monitor on the counter sounded with Gabe's cry.

"Want me to get him?" I asked her, but she shook her head and said she needed to feed him first. As Haley stood and began walking toward the stairs, I smacked her glorious ass, savoring the heady stare she sent my way.

It wasn't long before our family began arriving. Her father and Gina quickly followed by Tracy, and my brothers with their significant others. The only person missing was Tyler.

Haley joined us thirty minutes later with Gabe swaddled in her arms. The group all took chances fussing over him as they passed him around and gave him presents he wasn't going to use for years.

An hour later, Tyler rushed through the door, looking a bit distressed and he had dirt smudged on his arms and hands. My brothers made it a point to rag on him about it.

"Sorry," he said as he took a seat next to Mom.

"What happened?" I asked as I brought a beer out for him.

"I ran over someone when I was leaving campus."

Startled gasps echoed around the room, waking the now sleeping Gabe. Haley rushed over, took him out of the swing, and rocked him against her shoulder to calm him down.

"It was an accident. She was darting in and out of traffic carrying potted plants and dropped something in the middle of the street. She turned to go back for it without looking."

"Oh my gosh, Tyler," Mom admonished.

"She didn't want to involve the cops. So, I took her to the school clinic and she just had a couple of bruises. Now, can we eat?"

Once Gabe had settled, we took our seats at the large kitchen table Haley and I had purchased. Her father said a prayer for the family and I began to set the food out on the table.

We made small talk about Ford and Jolee's upcoming wedding and the teaching job Keeley had landed the past fall close to Wellington. Haley was still undecided if she wanted to go to work or stay at home with Gabe, but I was behind whichever decision she made.

Our family stayed until night had fallen and we'd watched *A Christmas Story* at least three times. Haley and I were lying on the couch together while Gabe snoozed in his bassinet close by.

"Did you think a year ago that this is where we'd be?" she asked me quietly.

"Not at all, but I'm not complaining. I couldn't have asked for anything better."

Haley turned over on the couch to face me; her head tucked safely against my chest. "Do you think about marriage and having more kids one day?"

It was all I could think about. Hell, I'd even considered making it official today, but she needed something special, memorable.

"All the time, cat. I think about it all the time, with you."

"I think about it too."

"We don't need to rush anything, we're still learning each other, but you're it for me. You're everything."

Gabe made a mewing sound from his bassinet and I lifted myself onto my hands to check on him. He wiggled and stuck his thumb in his mouth, quieting himself instantly. He was such a good baby.

I settled back onto the couch and tucked Haley's head back against my chest. She sighed in happiness.

How did I get so lucky?

STAY IN TOUCH

Newsletter: http://bit.ly/2WokAjS

Author Page: www.facebook.com/authorreneeharless

Reader Group: http://bit.ly/31AGa3B

Instagram: www.instagram.com/renee_harless

Bookbub: www.bookbub.com/authors/renee-harless

Goodreads: http://bit.ly/2TDagOn

Amazon: http://bit.ly/2WsHhPq

Website: www.reneeharless.com

ACKNOWLEDGMENTS

Thank you to all of the readers and bloggers that shared their excitement for this book and series. Rylan and Haley have spent four books building their relationship and I knew that it was going to be explosive when they came together. I couldn't wait to explore it more in Wicked Schemes.

Patricia, Lisa, and Paula thank you all so much for your help in making this book the best that it could be.

To the readers, thank you for taking a chance on this one. Although the accidental pregnancy trope isn't everyone's favorite, it's one of mine, and it really helped build the character's story.

To my family, thank you for the weekends and late nights that I needed to devote to Rylan and Haley. I love you all so much, every day, and I'm beyond thankful for your support.

ABOUT THE AUTHOR

Renee Harless is a romance writer with an affinity for wine and a passion for telling a good story.

Renee Harless, her husband, and children live in Blue Ridge Mountains of Virginia. She studied Communication, specifically Public Relations, at Radford University.

Growing up, Renee always found a way to pursue her creativity. It began by watching endless runs of White Christmas- yes even in the summer – and learning every word and dance from the movie. She could still sing "Sister Sister" if requested. In high school, she joined the show choir and a community theatre group, The Troubadours. After marrying the man of her dreams and moving from her hometown she sought out a different artistic outlet – writing.

To say that Renee is a romance addict would be an understatement. When she isn't chasing her kids around the house, working her day job, or writing, she jumps head first into a romance novel.

RENEE HARLESS